Check into the Pennyfoot Hotel . . .
for delightful tales of detection!

Room with a Clue
The view from the Pennyfoot's roof garden is lovely—but for Lady Eleanor Danbury, it was the last thing she ever saw. Now Cecily must find out who sent the snobbish society matron falling to her death . . .

Do Not Disturb
Mr. Bickley answered the door knocker and ended up dead. Cecily must capture the culprit—before murder darkens another doorway . . .

Service for Two
Dr. McDuff's funeral became a fiasco when the mourners found a stranger's body in the casket. Now Cecily must close the case—for at the Pennyfoot, murder is a most unwelcome guest . . .

Eat, Drink, and Be Buried
April showers bring May flowers—when one of the guests is found strangled with a maypole ribbon. Soon the May Day celebration turns into a hotel investigation—and Cecily fears it's a merry month . . . for murder.

Check-Out Time
Life at the Pennyfoot hangs in the balance one sweltering summer when a distinguished guest plunges to his death from his top-floor balcony. Was it the heat . . . or cold-blooded murder?

continued...

Grounds for Murder

The Pennyfoot's staff was put on edge when a young gypsy was hacked to death in the woods near Badgers End. And now it's up to Cecily to find out who at the Pennyfoot has a deadly ax to grind . . .

Pay the Piper

The Pennyfoot's bagpipe contest ended on a sour note when one of the pipers was murdered. Cecily must catch the killer—before another piper pays for his visit with his life . . .

Chivalry Is Dead

The jousting competition had everyone excited, until someone began early by practicing on—and murdering—Cecily's footman. Now she must discover who threw the lethal lance . . .

Ring for Tomb Service

St. Bartholomew's Week is usually one of Cecily's favorite times of the year. But this year, the celebration is marred by the unholiest of acts—murder . . .

Death with Reservations

When the doctor claims food poisoning killed a Pennyfoot guest, Cecily is suspicious. She'll have to do some investigating of her own—before death becomes the special of the day . . .

Dying Room Only

When a magician turns a vanishing act into murder, Cecily sets out to find the killer—and make him disappear for good . . .

MORE MYSTERIES FROM THE
BERKLEY PUBLISHING GROUP . . .

SISTER FREVISSE MYSTERIES: Medieval mystery in the tradition of Ellis Peters . . .

by Margaret Frazer

THE NOVICE'S TALE	THE SERVANT'S TALE	THE BOY'S TALE
THE OUTLAW'S TALE	THE BISHOP'S TALE	THE MURDERER'S TALE
THE PRIORESS' TALE	THE MAIDEN'S TALE	

PENNYFOOT HOTEL MYSTERIES: In Edwardian England, death takes a seaside holiday . . .

by Kate Kingsbury

ROOM WITH A CLUE	DO NOT DISTURB	PAY THE PIPER
SERVICE FOR TWO	EAT, DRINK, AND BE BURIED	CHIVALRY IS DEAD
CHECK-OUT TIME	GROUNDS FOR MURDER	RING FOR TOMB SERVICE
DEATH WITH RESERVATIONS	DYING ROOM ONLY	MAID TO MURDER

GLYNIS TRYON MYSTERIES: The highly acclaimed series set in the early days of the women's rights movement . . . "Historically accurate and telling."—Sara Paretsky

by Miriam Grace Monfredo

SENECA FALLS INHERITANCE	NORTH STAR CONSPIRACY	THE STALKING-HORSE
BLACKWATER SPIRITS	THROUGH A GOLD EAGLE	

MARK TWAIN MYSTERIES: "Adventurous . . . Replete with genuine tall tales from the great man himself."—*Mostly Murder*

by Peter J. Heck
DEATH ON THE MISSISSIPPI
A CONNECTICUT YANKEE IN CRIMINAL COURT
THE PRINCE AND THE PROSECUTOR

MAGGIE MAGUIRE MYSTERIES: A thrilling new series . . .

by Kate Bryan
MURDER AT BENT ELBOW
A RECORD OF DEATH
MURDER ON THE BARBARY COAST

MAID TO MURDER

KATE KINGSBURY

BERKLEY PRIME CRIME, NEW YORK

MAID TO MURDER

A Berkley Prime Crime Book / published by arrangement
with the author

PRINTING HISTORY
Berkley Prime Crime edition / July 1999

The Penguin Putnam Inc. World Wide Web site address is
http://www.penguinputnam.com

ISBN: 0-425-16967-7

Berkley Prime Crime Books are published
by The Berkley Publishing Group,
a division of Penguin Putnam Inc.,
375 Hudson Street, New York, New York 10014.
The name BERKLEY PRIME CRIME and the
BERKLEY PRIME CRIME design are trademarks
belonging to Penguin Putnam Inc.

PRINTED IN THE UNITED STATES OF AMERICA

10 9 8 7 6 5 4 3 2 1

MAID TO MURDER

CHAPTER

❧ 1 ❧

Summer came softly to Badgers End in the year of 1911. It was as if the entire English countryside mourned the passing of Edward VII, hushing the song of the lark and subduing the daisies that carpeted Putney Downs.

Cecily Sinclair could almost feel the melancholy in the salty air as she stood in the roof garden that sunny morning watching the silver ripples of a calm ocean.

Normally the opening of the Season held a festive air, a general bustling and hustling as the small town woke itself up from its long winter sleep and made ready for the influx of summer visitors.

This year was different, however. The beloved king of England, the playboy prince, was dead, and Cecily felt quite certain that something momentous had passed on with him. A glorious era, fueled by the ecstatic reign of a fun-loving, life-embracing king, was about to fade.

The evidence was everywhere. Reservations at the Pennyfoot Hotel were down significantly from last year. The staff were restless, as if aware of the drastic changes afoot. Some of the tiny gift shops along the esplanade remained boarded up, still awaiting their annual spring cleaning.

Caution, Cecily mused, as she watched a seagull glide effortlessly across the glittering water, its piercing gaze on the shallows where breakfast lurked unsuspecting. That's what she sensed all around her—an air of caution, as if everyone were waiting to see what was going to happen next.

"I hope *I* am not the cause of such a pensive expression."

The deep voice behind her startled her out of her thoughts. She spun around to face the smiling countenance of her manager. Baxter was now her partner in the hotel, but she still thought of him first and foremost as the man who had always kept the Pennyfoot running smoothly on well-oiled wheels.

As usual, looking upon Baxter's handsome face for the first time that day brought a rush of pleasure. "Quite the contrary, Baxter. It is only you who can chase away my gloomy thoughts."

His smile faded, and a sharpness gleamed in his gray eyes. "You are not ill, I hope? Have you received bad news? Michael? Andrew?"

Cecily shook her head, warmed beyond measure by his swift concern. "Both my sons are quite well, thank you. As far as I know, at least. I was merely contemplating the sense of change I feel in the air."

He came and stood beside her at the wall, his strong features composed as he gazed out to sea. "There are bound to be changes, Cecily. We have a new king."

"Yes. I can't help wondering what this reign will bring."

"Some things, I'm afraid, are inevitable. The talk of war in Europe, the workers rising up in arms against the people who put food on their tables, women rebelling in the streets . . ." He made a sound of disgust in his throat. "They are even invading the public bars nowadays. Can you imagine? Women—in a public bar. It should be against the law."

"Oh?"

She had spoken the word softly enough, but Baxter was well acquainted with her views and gave her a wary glance. "After all, there should be at least one small refuge where men can go to lick their wounds without having to curtail themselves because women happen to be present."

Cecily nodded, anticipating the coming exchange with concealed glee. "I see. By the term 'licking their wounds,' I assume you mean the abominable cursing, the obnoxious relating of dubious jokes, and the general disgusting behavior that men seem to enjoy when closeted in one of your precious public bars."

Baxter lifted his chin. "If you choose to put it that way. I have no intention of giving you the satisfaction of an argument on the subject."

"Very shrewd of you, Baxter, since you are perfectly aware that undoubtedly I should win."

One of his eyebrows twitched. "It is my considered opinion, my dear madam, that this country shows distinct signs of going to the dogs."

"Your usual definition of progress, I take it."

"If this is progress, I abhor it. All this modernization is turning the brains of our younger generation. Young people no longer show respect to their elders. They are loud, boorish, and turn our once peaceful roads into death traps with reckless driving of their motor cars. I have seen speeds surpassing fifteen miles per hour on the road to Wellercombe."

"And you would dearly love to join them."

"I would hope I have more respect for the safety of my fellow travelers. I have seen more than one mare rear up and bolt when terrified by the banging and rattling going on. London has become so noisy that it is difficult to make oneself heard above the racket."

Cecily studied him gravely. "Are you telling me, Baxter, that you wouldn't give your right arm to own one of those machines?"

Baxter stretched his neck and ran a finger around the inside of his starched white collar. "All I'm saying is that one should learn to be considerate when in charge of a dangerous vehicle. I dread to think what the future will bring if they start producing more powerful engines."

"I daresay we shall all learn to run faster."

He eyed her with suspicion. "You might view the situation with humor, Cecily, but I am deeply concerned about the future. Modern technology, if not handled with extreme care, could eventually destroy the world."

An uneasy stirring in her middle region made Cecily uncomfortable. "You would prefer the world to stagnate, is that it?"

"I would prefer to be assured that the future is in the hands of wise, intelligent men who are capable of controlling it."

"Well, thank you so much, Baxter. You have managed to turn my gloomy thoughts into deep depression."

He turned to her at once, his contrite expression reassuring her. "My dear madam, I humbly apologize. You are right, and that was quite the opposite of my intention. In fact, now that the opportunity has presented itself, I have something of great importance I wish to say to you."

"Not more bad news, I hope?" She was only half joking. Bad news had become a frequent visitor at the Pennyfoot of late. Sometimes she wondered how much more of it she could take.

What with the rising costs of running the hotel, the ever-increasing bills, the difficulty in hiring reliable staff, not to mention the unfortunate incidents that seemed to happen with alarming frequency, there were times when she felt like selling the place and forgetting she ever owned a hotel.

If it hadn't been for her promise to James, her long-dead husband, to keep the Pennyfoot in the family, she might well have put the hotel up for sale this summer.

"No, it isn't bad news. At least, I sincerely hope that you will not view it as such."

Something in his tone caught her attention. She narrowed

her eyes, staring into his face in an effort to read his thoughts. He appeared to be having some difficulty in deciding what it was he wanted to say. His face had lost its usual suave confidence. In fact, Baxter appeared to be greatly agitated about something.

In spite of his reassurance, her feeling of dread was like a cold hand on her heart. "Baxter, what is it? You are frightening me."

"I'm sorry, Cecily. I have no wish to do that. It is only that . . . after all this time . . . I . . ."

Thoroughly unnerved now, Cecily grasped his sleeve and gave it a little shake. "If you do not spit out the words this minute, I—"

"Cecily . . . dearest. I am trying to find the courage to ask you if you will do me the great honor of becoming my wife." His words ended on a little rush of breath.

Cecily snapped her mouth shut. After waiting . . . no . . . yearning for this moment for so long, she could hardly believe she'd actually heard him propose marriage. She felt quite faint and laid her hand on the wall behind her for support.

He stared at her, a faint flush staining his cheeks and a deep anxiety in his eyes. "I know I've thrust this upon you . . . Maybe this is an inopportune moment . . . Perhaps I should have . . . Oh, Lord . . ."

Her surge of love for him almost overwhelmed her. "Oh, for heaven's sake, Bax, stop babbling. I—"

Her words were interrupted by the loud slam of wood against brick as the attic door was flung open. Startled, Cecily stared at the newcomer. Daisy, a live-in nanny at the hotel, stood on the threshold, her cap askew and a wild look in her eyes that Cecily interpreted at once.

She'd seen enough bearers of bad tidings lately to know that Daisy wasn't there to pass the time of day. "What is it?" she demanded sharply. "What's happened now?"

Daisy obviously had difficulty answering. Her mouth slowly opened and closed like a goldfish waiting to be fed.

The fingers that clutched the frilled bodice of her apron showed white at the knuckles, and her cheeks, normally sporting a healthy ruddy glow, had taken on the color of Mrs. Chubb's bread dough.

Apparently sensing Cecily's concern, Baxter strode over to the girl and shook her arm. "What is it, child? Speak up."

"Oh, mum . . . Mr. Baxter, sir, it's awful, that's what it is. I've never seen such an 'orrible sight in me entire life. That I haven't." Tears spurted from Daisy's eyes and rushed down her pallid cheeks.

Alarmed, Cecily rushed forward and took the girl's hands in hers. In spite of the balmy temperature, they were ice cold. "It's all right, Daisy, take your time. Tell us what you saw."

Daisy gulped and made an obvious effort to control the embarrassing tears. It was the first time Cecily had ever seen the young girl cry, unlike her twin sister, Doris, whose job as a kitchen maid in the hotel often had her dissolving into tears at the slightest provocation.

For a moment Cecily wondered if Doris was the cause of her twin's unexpected weakness. Doris had recently left the Pennyfoot to live in London, and Cecily was well aware of how much Daisy missed her sister. In fact, it crossed her mind that Daisy's outburst might well be due to the fact that she was attempting to give in her notice.

Daisy's next words, however, proved her decisively wrong. "It's Flora, mum. I found her in one of the bathrooms, I did. O-o-h-h, it was awful, it was." The last word ended on a high pitched wail.

Baxter gave Cecily a puzzled look. "Flora?"

"The new maid. Remember? We hired three of them a month ago. Flora, Emily, and . . . Pansy, I think. They started work yesterday. Mrs. Chubb was going to send them to you first, but they've been so busy getting things ready—" She broke off as Daisy almost choked on a sob. "I'm sorry, Daisy. Please try to calm yourself and tell us what you saw. Is Flora ill or something?"

Daisy's lip trembled, but the tears dried on her cheeks. "Not ill, mum. Flora's . . . dead."

"Dead!"

"Oh, no!"

Baxter and Cecily both spoke at once, and Daisy violently nodded her head.

"It's true, mum. I seen her lying there. I was going in there to put new soap in the dishes, and there she was . . . lying in the tub . . ."

"She was in the tub?" Baxter's voice was sharp when he questioned the frightened girl. "Are you quite sure she was dead and not just unconscious?" He glanced at Cecily. "I'd better take a look."

"No!" Daisy's hand came out involuntarily and was just as quickly withdrawn. Her eyes pleaded with Cecily as she muttered, "You'll have to go, mum. Flora's . . . well, she's . . ."

"She's what, girl? What are you trying to say?"

Daisy looked down at the ground, tracing a line in the dust with the toe of her polished Oxford shoe. "She's undressed, mum."

"Undressed?" Cecily frowned. "She was taking a bath in the tub? Didn't anyone tell her that the bathrooms are for the exclusive use of the guests and the staff are not permitted to use them?"

"Yes, mum." Daisy nodded her head as if she were being manipulated by a puppeteer. "I told her myself, I did. But I don't know as if she were taking a bath, mum. Though her clothes were folded in a neat pile by her side."

Baxter cursed quietly under his breath. "The girl has probably fallen asleep. Tell Mrs. Chubb to take care of her."

Daisy looked up. "She ain't . . . isn't asleep, Mr. Baxter. She choked to death."

"Choked?" Baxter looked stunned. "On what?"

"On account of the stocking what's wound around her neck."

Cecily felt as if a rain barrel had been emptied on her

head. A moment or two passed before she could speak. Even Baxter seemed to be at a loss for words.

"It weren't me what done it, mum, honest," Daisy said, beginning to cry again. "I don't have nothing to do with the maids as a rule. I was only helping out 'cause they're so slow, and all, and Mrs. Chubb asked me as a special favor . . ."

"It's all right, Daisy." Cecily drew in a long breath. "Have you told anyone else about this?"

Daisy shook her head. "I locked the bathroom so as no one could get in there." She fished in the pocket of her apron and drew out a key. Holding it out to Cecily, she muttered, "I couldn't let them all gawk at poor Flora's naked body, now could I?"

Baxter cleared his throat, and Cecily said quickly, "You did the right thing, Daisy. Where are the babies? Aren't you supposed to be looking after them?"

"Yes, I am, mum. They was sleeping when I left, but I'd better get back to them, hadn't I."

"As quickly as possible." Cecily managed a smile of encouragement. "Try not to think about all this if you can. Mr. Baxter and I will take care of things."

"Yes, mum." Daisy dropped a small curtsey and turned to go.

"Oh, I'd rather you didn't say anything to anyone about this, Daisy." Cecily glanced at Baxter. "At least until we've had a chance to find out what happened."

"All right, mum, I won't. I just feel sorry for her. She was only thirteen. This was her very first job."

"I know, Daisy. It's very sad." Cecily's stomach felt as if it were full of stones. She would have to deal with yet another catastrophe. There had been so many at the Pennyfoot. How much longer could the hotel survive in the wake of such tragedy?

"Funny thing," Daisy said, looking back over her shoulder as she stepped back through the door. "I noticed one of

Flora's shoes were missing. What do you think could have happened to it?"

"I can't imagine." Cecily wished she could simply lean against Baxter's solid warmth and wish this latest nightmare away. "Rest assured we'll find out, though."

"Yes, mum." Daisy's face was somber as she quietly closed the door behind her.

After making quite sure they were alone again, Cecily turned to her grave-looking manager. "I had better go down there and find out what happened."

"I'll come with you." He held the door open for her and waited for her to precede him down the narrow staircase. "There's always the possibility that this is all an elaborate prank, you know."

Cecily didn't answer him. Somehow she just couldn't bring herself to believe that a new maid of Flora's tender years would play such an ambitious prank the first week of her very first job.

It seemed much more likely that the thing she dreaded most had happened again. Once more an innocent victim had lost her life by a violent hand in the Pennyfoot Hotel.

"Gertie? Gert-a-y! Wake up, will you!" The voice of Mrs. Chubb, the Pennyfoot's formidable housekeeper, rang out across the kitchen, making Gertie jump so hard she dropped the sherry decanter she'd been holding. The fragile glass splintered as the vessel crashed into the sink, spraying shards in all directions.

"Now look what you've bleeding made me do!" Gertie began mopping up the pieces with the damp tea towel she'd used to dry the glasses.

"Leave it be," Mrs. Chubb ordered, glaring at Gertie out of her beady little eyes. "I'll get Samuel to clean it up. I need you to get out into that dining room and help Pansy to set up those tables. The guests will be down to breakfast any minute now."

"What guests? We've only got two dozen or so people in

the entire bloody place." Gertie dropped the towel and wiped her hands on her apron.

"They still have to be fed and waited on, and none of those new maids know what they're doing yet. Someone has to show them how."

"So why does it bleeding have to be me, that's what I want to know?"

"Because with Doris in London and Ethel gone to the sanitarium, you're the only one left to show them, that's why." Mrs. Chubb picked up her wooden spoon and waved it at Gertie. "Now stop arguing with me and get out there. And straighten that cap. I don't know why you can't look neat and tidy like the rest of the staff."

"*Sacre bleu!*" The exclamation was accompanied by a loud crashing of a saucepan lid as Michel, the tall, lanky chef, swept an arm across the stove. " 'Ow can I concentrate with all this racket going on, I ask you? Where is ze cream I ask for? You are waiting for ze cow to bring it, *oui*?"

Gertie wrinkled her nose at the irate man. She was used to Michel's tantrums and took little notice of them. The only time she was wary of the chef was when he'd sampled too much of the kitchen brandy, and she always knew when that happened because he forgot to speak with his French accent. Michel was about as bleeding French as she was Queen Victoria.

"Gertie, I swear, if you don't get out there this instant . . ."

"Cor, strewth." Gertie lifted her hands in the air and glared at the housekeeper in disgust. "I never worked this flipping hard when I was a bleeding kitchen maid."

"Then get out there and teach those new girls what to do." Mrs. Chubb slapped at a fly that had the audacity to settle on her generous hip.

"All right, I'm going. Don't get your bleeding knickers in a twist." Gertie reached the door just as it swung open. She had no time to get out of the way as the young man barrelled straight into her.

Gertie was built like a house, broad and big-boned, but the wiry weight of Samuel, the hotel's stable manager, was enough to slam all the air out of her lungs.

A torrent of curses formed in her mind, but fortunately she was unable to deliver them. She could only stand there and fight for breath as Samuel, cap twisting in his hands, came to a full stop in the middle of the kitchen without so much as an apology.

Mrs. Chubb looked a little put out, but her reprimand was cut off by Samuel's agitated voice.

"It's happened again," he said hoarsely.

"What's happened?" Mrs. Chubb crossed her arms over her copious bosom.

"Murder." Samuel dropped his voice to an eerie whisper. "One of them new maids has been murdered."

Having finally found her breath, Gertie dropped three succinct words into the shocked silence. "Bloody flipping hell."

CHAPTER

🕸 2 🕸

"I say, old chap, this glass looks half empty." Colonel Fortescue held up his gin and stared accusingly at Martin, the Pennyfoot's bartender.

Being well acquainted with the colonel's eccentricities, Martin gave him a bland smile. "Yes, sir. That's because you've already drank half of it, sir."

The colonel stared down at the glass in his hand in astonishment. "I did? By Jove, that went down blasted fast. You're quite sure someone else didn't drink it?"

"Quite sure, Colonel. After all, you are the only person in here."

Fortescue's bloodshot eyes swiveled in their sockets as he sent a hazy glance around the room. "Dashed if you're not right, old chap. Must be getting a little addled in the old noggin, what? What?"

In Martin's opinion, the portly old gentleman's brain had

been beyond help for a good many years, but he held his tongue. Fortescue was a regular guest at the Pennyfoot, and Mrs. Sinclair had made it clear to the entire staff that no matter how outrageous the colonel's antics became, he was to be treated with the utmost respect.

There had been times when Fortescue's behavior had bordered on lunacy, but so far everyone had managed to handle the situation and avoid alarming the other guests.

Though Martin had to admit, lately the colonel seemed to have calmed down a great deal. No doubt the influence of Phoebe Carter-Holmes had an effect on him. As ludicrous as the idea seemed, that good lady appeared to have formed an attachment to the crazy old coot.

Martin shook his head as he wiped down the polished mahogany counter. To each his own. What with the colonel being a bachelor, and Mrs. Carter-Holmes a widow, what was the harm in a little hanky panky now and again? Martin almost choked at the thought.

"Did you say something, old bean?"

Martin straightened his face at once. "No, sir. Just clearing my throat, that was all."

"Ah." Fortescue nodded. "I remember when I was out in Africa . . . Boer War, you know."

Here it comes, Martin thought gloomily. Once the colonel got started on his war stories, there was no stopping him. Not until he'd finally downed enough booze to put him to sleep, in any case.

"Anyway, there I was, out in that blasted sun, when—"

Martin looked up as the colonel's voice cut off midstream. Someone else had entered the room, and Martin could see why the colonel appeared to be dumfounded. He was a little shaken up himself.

The gentleman who had just walked in and was now taking a seat at the bar was a carbon copy of Fortescue. Right down to the beer belly, thick white hair, bushy eyebrows, and twirled mustache. They could have been brothers.

"I say, old chap," Fortescue muttered, "when did you put that mirror in here?"

The newcomer uttered a hearty laugh and held out his hand. "Chatsworth's the name, old man. Brigadier Albert Chatsworth. Retired, of course."

Fortescue's eyelids began furiously flapping up and down, a sure sign that he was agitated. He fumbled a salute and struggled to climb off the high bar stool. "An honor to meet you, sir. Excuse me for not recognizing you right away. Sir."

Chatsworth shook his head. "No, no, old man. We've never met, as far as I can recall."

The colonel, having finally floundered to his feet, drew himself up to his full height. "Colonel Frederick Fortescue, sir. Her Majesty's Army Corps, Infantry Division. Sir!"

"At ease, Colonel." Looking past Fortescue's shoulder, Chatsworth winked at Martin. "Fill this man's glass with whatever he's drinking, and pour me a double Scotch."

"Right away, sir." Martin busied himself with the drinks, though his full attention was on the men at the bar. He couldn't get over the likeness. They were almost identical, except for the way they dressed. The brigadier's conservative dark suit was in startling contrast to the colonel's loudly checkered coat and tweed knickerbockers.

"Do sit down, Fortescue, there's a good fellow." Chatsworth's voice held just an edge of condescension.

The colonel, never remiss at seizing an opportunity, reached for his glass and drained it before handing it over to Martin to be refilled. Seating himself, he grinned rather foolishly at the brigadier. "Jolly decent of you, sir. Much obliged, I'm sure. Sir."

Chatsworth sighed. "No need to call me 'sir' either. I left all that behind when I retired. Let's just forget we were ever in the army, all right?"

Martin shot a look at the colonel. Fortescue's eyes looked as if they were bulging out of his head. "Forget we were in the army? I say, old bean, that's not cricket, what? Dashed proud to have served in Her Majesty's Forces. So should you be. Sir. If I might say so.''

"Yes, well, it's not Her Majesty any longer, is it."

The colonel looked confused. "It's not?"

Chatsworth sent a hunted look at Martin. Not knowing what else to do, Martin responded by lightly tapping his forehead and winking.

Chatsworth's expression changed as understanding dawned. Softening his tone, he said mildly, "We've had a king for the past ten years, old man. It's His Majesty's Forces now, so I think we can dispense with all the formality, don't you? It isn't even our army anymore."

"By Jove." Fortescue looked gloomily at the glass of gin Martin handed to him. "Dashed rotten luck, that, what?"

"Precisely."

Martin hid a grin as Chatsworth rolled his eyes at him.

Fortescue downed his gin and set the glass on the counter. "Good drop of mother's ruin, that."

"Care for another?"

The colonel's face lit up like the beach on Guy Fawkes night. "Oh, I say, old chap. Don't mind if I do. Dashed decent of you, and all that, what?"

"My pleasure." The brigadier signaled Martin for a refill.

"What outfit were you in, then, Chatsworth? Hey?"

For a moment the brigadier looked startled. "Oh, same as you. Africa, actually. Boer War."

"By George, so was I. Whereabouts?

"Er . . . Mafeking." Chatsworth lifted his hands to adjust the knot of his tie. "So where do you live now, then, Fortescue?"

The colonel looked excited. "I say, this is extraordinary. You must have been at Hussar Hill, then."

Chatsworth cleared his throat. "Yes, yes. I was. Down for a spot of relaxation, are you?"

"Perishing bastards nearly got me there. Got the chappie right next to me. Dropped like a stone. I just kept going, of course. Poor blighter."

"Down from London, I'll wager."

Fortescue abandoned the topic of the Boer War with obvious reluctance. "Yes, old chap. Kensington. Not the city it used to be, what?"

Chatsworth nodded. "Indeed. Married?"

"Not yet, sir. Never had time while I was in the army. Getting ready to take the plunge, though."

Martin's ears pricked up.

"Really?" Chatsworth chuckled. "Found yourself a little filly, what?"

"That I have. Dashed fine woman. Got a pair of—"

Martin winced.

Mercifully the colonel was interrupted by Baxter, who hurried into the room looking somewhat harried. "Ah, there you are, Fortescue." He caught sight of the colonel's companion and was visibly startled. "Good Lord."

Chatsworth's hand wandered to his tie again as he warily eyed the hotel manager. "I beg your pardon?"

Baxter recovered his usual composure. "Excuse me, sir. You wouldn't be Brigadier Chatsworth, by any chance?"

"I was when I got up this morning." Chatsworth laughed heartily at his own joke.

Fortescue, not to be outdone, joined in. "Jolly good, old boy." Turning to Baxter, he said with a trace of scorn, "Of course he's the brigadier, my good man. You can tell he's an army man just by looking at him. Saw action in blasted Mafeking, same time I was there, what?" He nudged the brigadier's arm so forcefully his Scotch spilled across the counter.

Chatsworth's smile died, and Baxter frowned. "Yes, well, as long as I have you both here, I should inform you that the bathroom on the second floor is out of order for the time being. You will have to confine your use to the remaining two bathrooms on the first and third floors until we get things sorted out. Bit of a nuisance, I'm afraid."

"Oh, that's all right, old man." Chatsworth drained what was left in his glass and got off his stool. "Done far worse in the tropics, what?'' Grinning at Fortescue, he nudged him, none too gently, in the shoulder.

Whether it was done purposefully as a counterattack, Martin couldn't be sure. One thing was certain, it took the colonel completely by surprise. Already somewhat unsteady, due to the gin he'd consumed, he lost his balance and toppled off the stool.

By the time Martin and Baxter had helped Fortescue to his feet and restored order, Chatsworth had disappeared.

''I can't believe it. That poor child.'' Mrs. Chubb sat huddled at the kitchen table, her face buried in her apron.

Gertie felt awkward. It wasn't often the housekeeper gave in to her emotions. In fact, it was so rare that when it did happen, it rocked Gertie's secure world.

''It were Daisy what found her,'' Samuel said, obviously pleased with the sensation he was causing. ''In the bathtub. Stark naked with a stocking wrapped around her neck. She'd been strangled.''

There was a loud gasp from the doorway, and Gertie spun around to face the two novice maids huddled together in the doorway.

''Get in here, you blithering idiots,'' she ordered, glad of the excuse to vent some of her anxiety. ''You want everyone in the bleeding hotel to know what's going on?''

''Who got strangled, then?'' Pansy asked, the taller of the two. She had the kind of fragile features and silky jet black hair that would turn her into a beauty one day.

Gertie was well aware that she would never attain such desirable heights, but for once it didn't bother her. That very afternoon the man of her dreams was due to arrive at the Pennyfoot to take up the position of hotel gardener, and Gertie couldn't wait to see him again.

Ross McBride had proposed a year ago, and she had turned him down. She hadn't expected to hear from him again after he'd returned to his native Scotland, but his letters had arrived on a regular basis. When she had mentioned to him that Mrs. Sinclair was looking for a new gardener, much to Gertie's surprise, Ross had applied and had been accepted.

Her stomach got all squiggly every time she thought about hearing his deep, husky voice again. Fair gave her shivers, it did. She'd been practicing hard all week to stop swearing, a habit that was as natural to her as breathing. Since every other word she used was the wrong word, her sentences were coming out choppy.

All this excitement today had undone much of the progress she'd achieved, and she glared at the maids as if it were their fault. "It were Flora what got bl—strangled, that's what."

Emily promptly burst into tears, while Pansy stared at her, white-faced.

"Gertie!" Recovering her indomitable spirit, Mrs. Chubb rose from her chair like an avenging angel. "That's no way to break such dreadful news. Flora was their friend."

"No, she weren't." Pansy tossed her head. "She just started with us, that's all. We never knew each other before yesterday."

"I want my mum," Emily sobbed.

"Well, you can't go home," Pansy said loftily. "We're working girls now, and we're stuck with it, so there. You've got to act grown up. Doesn't she, Miss Brown?"

Gertie sighed. Part of her felt sorry for the poor little bugger. She could still remember how she felt when she first came to the Pennyfoot. Alone, afraid, overwhelmed by the hugeness of the place, and hiding it all behind a defiant attitude and a barrage of swear words. "Even grown-ups cry sometimes," she said gruffly.

Fishing in the pocket of her apron, she found the large man's handkerchief she'd carried ever since she'd cleared out her home when Ian had left her three years ago. Handing it to Emily, she added, "Dry your blinking tears, then, and get some water out of the rain barrel to wash your face."

Emily took the handkerchief and gave her a wavering

smile of gratitude. "Thank you, Miss Brown."

Gertie tried not to notice the warm feeling that smile gave her. She turned her attention instead to Samuel, who stood talking earnestly to an enraptured Mrs. Chubb. Even Michel had stopped his crashing around to listen.

"Anyway, all I know is they found her clothes all piled up by the side of the bath, and one shoe missing."

Mrs. Chubb looked shocked. "One shoe? Whatever would someone want one shoe for?"

"Maybe he's only got one foot," Pansy piped up. "All you have to do is find someone with a wooden leg and you'll know who strangled Flora."

Gertie looked at her with new respect. The maid seemed unaffected by the news, even excited about it. The girl had nerve, and Gertie admired anyone who could take care of herself without having to rely on a man to do it for her. Pansy, it seemed, was that kind of girl.

Samuel apparently didn't share Gertie's admiration. He uttered a derisive laugh. "What are you going to do, then, take his wooden leg and hit him with it?"

Pansy pouted. "Don't be silly. Anyhow, I bet I know who did it."

Five pairs of eyes fastened on her pert face.

"Who, then?" Samuel demanded, sounding less sure of himself.

"That weird man what keeps muttering about the world coming to an end."

"What weird man?" Mrs. Chubb marched across the kitchen floor and stood in front of Pansy with her arms crossed. "You'd better not be making this up, my girl."

Pansy's face flushed, but she stood her ground. "I'm not making it up, Mrs. Chubb. Honest, I'm not. I've bumped into him twice, I have. Both times he told me the world was coming to an end. Gave me the creeps he did."

Gertie felt her skin shiver. They didn't need this trouble at the hotel, what with Ross starting work tomorrow. She wanted everything to be perfect for him, so that he'd stay and not want to go back to Scotland without her again.

"Well, he's probably one of the guests having a bit of fun," Mrs. Chubb declared. "What did he look like?"

Pansy shrugged. "He had strange eyes, with huge black circles underneath them, and a beard what covered half his face."

"A big man?"

"Nah. Little. Shorter than Samuel even."

"He's probably long gone by now," Mrs. Chubb said with a confidence Gertie wished she shared. "He won't hang around now that he's done the murder."

"Here!" Apparently insulted by the implication that he was short, Samuel glared at her.

"Oh, give over, Samuel," Gertie said, winking at Pansy. "Everyone knows you walk on tiptoes to look taller."

"That's a lie—"

A loud crash made them all turn to look at Michel, who stood surrounded by the three pans he'd just flung on the floor. "*Mon Dieu!*" he roared. "When do we get ze breakfast, then? Or per'aps you tie feed bags of straw under ze chins of our guests, like ze horses, *oui*?"

"Keep your bleeding hair on," Gertie muttered. "Come on, Pansy. I'll help you finish the tables." She followed the girl out of the door, thankful to leave all the racket behind as Mrs. Chubb raised her voice to override Michel's furious tirade.

Poor Ross, she thought as she stomped down the long hallway to the dining room. What a mess he was coming into. In spite of Samuel's assurances she didn't feel too safe knowing a murderer could still be lurking around the hotel.

Now she couldn't wait for Ross to get there. Much as she hated to admit it, she would feel a good deal safer knowing a burly Scotsman was around who would be only too happy to take care of her.

Amazed at her own change of attitude, she followed the slim figure of the new maid into the dining room. It had been a whole year since she'd last seen him. Things could have changed in that time. She smiled, wondering what Ross would think of James and Lilly, her twins. Almost three they were now, and a bleeding handful. If it weren't for Daisy taking care of them, she'd never be able to work in the hotel.

They'd never known what it was like to have a father. She'd never told Ian she was pregnant. The day she'd found out he already had a wife and wasn't really married to her, she'd shut him out of her life forever. He had no idea he was the father of twins.

Nor would he ever know, she vowed silently. The twins were hers, and they didn't need a father. They had Mr. Baxter, their godfather, and Samuel, who played with them whenever he got the chance, and now they'd have Ross, too.

The warm feeling spread throughout her entire body, and she felt like hugging herself. Ross was coming back today. And she couldn't wait to see him.

CHAPTER
3

"Dr. Prestwick will be arriving very shortly," Baxter informed Cecily as she sat at the long library table sorting out her notes for the committee meeting that morning. In spite of the latest catastrophe, life at the hotel had to go on, and the opening of the summer season always began with a grand ball in the ballroom.

In spite of the lack of guests that week, Cecily was determined that the ball should be held as usual. She was expecting her two committee members, Phoebe Carter-Holmes and Madeline Pengrath, to arrive any minute, and she wanted to be well prepared.

The meetings had a tendency to get out of hand, thanks to the bickering between her two friends, and it helped to have everything in order. Otherwise, too much time was wasted in getting back to the preparations of the ball.

As always, Baxter's voice had held a note of disapproval.

She was well aware that her partner did not care for the doctor's charming attitude toward the ladies, herself in particular. There had been a time when the good doctor had actively pursued her. The fact that Kevin Prestwick no longer paid her such close attention had apparently escaped Baxter's notice. Wisely choosing not to comment on the subject, however, Cecily merely nodded.

Baxter moved over to the fireplace and stood with his back to it, hands clasped behind him. "Nasty business this. She was little more than a child."

Cecily tried not to think about the sight of that frail body lying limp and lifeless in the bathtub. "This is not a good start to the season, is it? I dread to think how this will affect our guests. Bookings are so dismal this year already. If we lose any more customers we'll be forced to close down for a while."

"I suppose it's too much to hope we can keep it quiet."

"Hopeless, I'm afraid. Once the constable appears on the scene, everyone will know something is amiss, and word spreads so quickly. I assume Police Constable Northcott is on his way?"

Baxter pursed his lips. "I left a message for him."

"Well, thank heavens we don't have many guests. With any luck, word of this latest catastrophe will not be spread around too far."

"Which reminds me." Baxter walked over to the table and sat down on one of the chairs. "I saw that Chatsworth fellow in the bar, talking to Fortescue."

"Chatsworth?"

"The brigadier, remember? Retired, I should say. Apparently he was in the same outfit as Fortescue."

"Oh, dear," Cecily murmured, shuffling her notes into a neat pile. "I can just imagine their conversation. A total reenactment of the Boer War, no doubt, complete with sound effects."

Baxter smiled. "Not exactly. But the odd thing is, Chatsworth looks exactly like the colonel. They could be twins."

"Really? You mean there are two of them? That should provide some entertainment. Maybe they will distract the guests' minds enough to forget about the murder."

"I don't know about entertainment. I don't think the brigadier is too amused by Fortescue's antics. In fact, he knocked him off the stool."

Cecily stared at him. "No! You can't mean it."

"Well, it really wasn't all that difficult, in view of the fact that Fortescue had swallowed his usual allotment of gin. One could have dusted him with a feather, and he would have fallen off that stool. I don't think Chatsworth really meant to send him flying."

"Is he all right?"

Baxter solemnly nodded. "I doubt he ever knew what hit him. Probably believes he toppled off there all by himself."

"Even so—"

"Have you given any thought to my proposal?

The abrupt question took her by surprise. "We—yes, as a matter of fact—"

She broke off as Baxter raised his hand. "Don't tell me now. I want to do this properly. On bended knee and all that. In the roof garden. It's your favorite spot in the entire hotel, and I want you to remember it forever. Even if the answer is 'no.' "

As if she could possibly refuse him. And as if he didn't know that. Her rush of tenderness almost overwhelmed her. "Why, Baxter," she managed to say lightly, "how very romantic of you."

"So, would you care to meet me in the roof garden, say, in an hour?"

"I'd be delighted. Will you pick a rose for me?"

Before he could answer, a light tap on the door interrupted him. He rose immediately, smoothing back his hair in an automatic gesture before moving to the door.

Emily stood in the doorway, her thin fingers nervously twisting her apron as she bobbed a curtsey. "Excuse me, mum, Mrs. Chubb said to tell you the doctor has arrived. He's waiting in the drawing room.''

"Thank you, Emily." Cecily gave the girl an encouraging smile. "We'll be right along."

"Yes, mum." Emily backed out of the room and fled down the hall.

"That's one of the new maids, I take it," Baxter said, crossing the room to pull back Cecily's chair.

"Yes. Nice little girl, though dreadfully shy." Cecily rose gracefully to her feet. "Pansy, the third girl, has a lot more gumption. She should do well here."

The door opened suddenly, preceded by the barest of taps, and a willowy woman with long, flowing black hair drifted into the room.

"I hope I'm not interrupting anything?" Madeline asked hopefully with a sly glance at Baxter.

Cecily smiled. "As a matter of fact, I was just leaving to talk to Dr. Prestwick." Her long-time friend was one of the few people who knew about her true relationship with Baxter, and Madeline made no secret of the fact that she enjoyed the intrigue immensely.

Madeline gave her a sharp look. "You're not ill or anything, are you? If so, I have some wonderful new remedies that will take care of just about anything."

Cecily glanced at Baxter, knowing how he felt about Madeline's prowess with her herb and wildflower remedies. He regarded the woman, as did most of the villagers, as a sorceress, whose strange powers were capable of turning people into insects at the flick of a finger.

Cecily, of course, knew better, though there had been times when Madeline's unique talents had baffled even her logical mind. "Thank you, Madeline," she said, hurrying forward before Baxter could utter one of his terse comments, "but I'm quite well, as you can see. I'm afraid, though, that we have some rather disturbing news. One of our new maids was found strangled in one of the bathrooms early this morning.''

Madeline's beautiful brown eyes clouded with shock. "I had no idea. Is there anything I can do?"

Cecily regarded her thoughtfully. Madeline's second sight had proved rather useful in the past, though it was inclined to be unpredictable at best. "I suppose you could take a look," she said slowly. "Dr. Prestwick is here to examine the body, but I don't think he'll have any objections."

Madeline wrinkled her nose. "He always has objections. He doesn't approve of my methods for curing ills."

"I wonder why?" Baxter murmured with a trace of sarcasm.

Madeline sent him a dark look. "I keep reminding him that my herb remedies were curing people long before all his modern technology came into being."

"Well, I'm sure he's willing to give you the benefit of the doubt," Cecily said hurriedly.

She turned to Baxter, who was hovering near the doorway. "Baxter, Phoebe will be arriving shortly. Would you mind awfully waiting for her and explaining what happened? Madeline and I shouldn't be too long. Perhaps you could arrange for a tea tray . . . you know how Phoebe adores our little pastries."

Baxter gave her a look that said he minded very much, but then he inclined his head and opened the door for her to pass through, followed by Madeline.

"When is that man ever going to declare his intentions?" Madeline demanded as she floated alongside Cecily down the long hallway. "If he doesn't get to it soon, you'll either be too old or you will have found someone else. Doesn't he realize the precious time he's wasting?"

Taken by surprise, Cecily couldn't think of a thing to say.

As she expected, Madeline took one look at her face and stopped short. "Cecily! Don't tell me he's already done it?"

Sighing, Cecily came to a halt. "Madeline, it's much too soon to talk about it."

Madeline's lovely face was brimming with excitement. "But why?"

"Because I haven't given him an answer yet. And if you dare breathe a word and embarrass me, I'll never forgive you."

Madeline's lilting laugh echoed down the corridor. "Don't worry, Cecily darling, my lips are sealed. But how terribly delicious! You are going to say 'yes,' of course. How wonderful. A September wedding?"

"I don't know. I can't think about that now with this dreadful murder hanging over us. I'm afraid my personal life will have to wait until whoever did this is safely behind bars."

"Well, you can rely on me to say nothing . . . on one condition."

Cecily regarded her friend warily. "What's that?"

"That I'm invited to the wedding."

"I wouldn't dream of getting married without you there," Cecily promised her.

Satisfied at last, Madeline accompanied her to the drawing room, where Dr. Prestwick paced up and down with obvious impatience.

The doctor looked immaculate, as always, in a neat pin-striped suit and crisp white shirt. His bowler, gloves and umbrella rested on an armchair by the fireplace, and a thick, gold watch chain dangled from his waistcoat pocket.

"Cecily!" he cried when the two ladies entered the room. "You are looking utterly ravishing, as always." Reaching for Cecily's hands, he pressed a kiss on her fingers, then turned to Madeline.

His gaze swept rather boldly over her pale blue gauze dress before he bowed low over her hand. "Miss Pengrath. As delectable as ever, I see."

"Dr. Prestwick," Madeline murmured in response.

Cecily was intrigued to see a faint flush color her friend's cheeks. It wasn't often Madeline was disconcerted by a man. "Kevin," Cecily said, turning to smile ruefully at the doctor, "I wish it were for any other reason that you were summoned to the Pennyfoot."

"Whatever the reason," Prestwick said smoothly, "it is always a pleasure to enjoy your delightful company. I trust Baxter is well?"

"Very well, thank you."

"He is a lucky man. But then, he must be well aware of that."

Well used to the doctor's effusive flattery—after all, he didn't get his reputation as a ladies' man without some justification—Cecily passed off the comment. "If you'll come with me, I'll show you where the poor girl is lying. We thought it best not to disturb anything."

"Quite right." Prestwick nodded, adopting a more formal air. "I take it Northcott is on the way?"

The resigned note in his voice made Cecily smile. P. C. Northcott was not known for his alacrity or expertise. "He has indicated that he'll be along later. I'm hoping we can discover who is responsible for this dreadful deed before Inspector Cranshaw puts in an appearance. Whenever that gentleman visits the Pennyfoot, it's usually to inform me he is about to shut down the hotel."

Prestwick shook his head. "I'm sorry, Cecily. You do seem to have more than your fair share of problems here lately."

"Well, this is one of the worst of them. To lose one of my staff like that. It has happened before, and it is always very difficult. . . ." She let her voice trail off, afraid it might break.

Madeline's arm rested briefly about her shoulders. "I'll be happy to accompany Dr. Prestwick to the bathroom if you're not up to it."

Cecily straightened her back. "Thank you, Madeline. I shall be fine. Though I would like you to accompany us, if Dr. Prestwick has no objection?"

Prestwick's appraisal of Madeline's lithe body was again frank and quite audacious. "Not at all. I shall be delighted to be in such pleasurable company. Just as long as you don't want to sprinkle dried blossoms everywhere."

Instead of the sharp retort she expected, Cecily was
stunned when Madeline tossed her head, allowing her silky
black hair to settle over her shoulders before saying with a
distinct note of coquetry, "Why, Doctor, please don't tell
me you have a distaste for rose petals?"

Prestwick eyed her with a faint smile. "I can assure you,
Miss Pengrath, in the right place and at the right time, I
would find rose petals quite devastating."

For answer, Madeline slowly and deliberately lifted her
hand and smoothed her long hair over her bosom.

Cecily felt her mouth drop open and hastily closed it. She
had heard many tales about Madeline's magnetism over the
opposite sex, but she'd never actually seen her friend in action, so to speak.

Prestwick looked as if someone had whisked him away
and deposited him in an enchanted fairyland. The man
looked positively besotted. There was no doubt that Madeline knew what she was about. Cecily had never seen Kevin
Prestwick lose the upper hand so effectively.

Could there be something brewing between the two of
them? If so, Cecily was determined to find out. Promising
herself that she would tackle her friend at the earliest opportunity, she said firmly, "I think we had better move to
that bathroom if you want to be finished before the constable
arrives."

Prestwick blinked and snapped back to normal at once.
"Of course. Shall we go, then? If you wouldn't mind leading
the way, Cecily?"

Putting him directly beside Madeline, of course, Cecily
thought caustically. Not that she ever took any notice of
Prestwick's compliments, but she did rather miss his attention at times.

Scolding herself for such an immature thought, she led the
way up to the second floor and along the hall to the bathroom. Taking Daisy's key from her pocket, she unlocked the
door and threw it open. Fortunately what few guests there
were would be out on the sands at this hour. They should

be relatively undisturbed, she thought, as Prestwick stooped over the bathtub to examine the body.

Cecily turned away, not wishing to remind herself again of the once pretty girl's swollen, discolored face. Madeline patted her on the shoulder, though her attention appeared to be fixed on the doctor's confident hands.

Madeline had once confessed to Cecily that had things been different in her life, she would have liked to be a doctor. She certainly had the right qualifications—the caring, the understanding, as well as the desire and the ability to heal.

It struck Cecily, quite forcibly, that Madeline would make a wonderful partner for Kevin Prestwick. It was high time they both settled down. Excited at the thought, she managed to keep her mind off what was taking place in the bathtub.

Finally the doctor straightened, reaching for a dazzling white towel hanging from the rail. "That should do it, I think. At least until I can get the corpse down to my office."

Cecily swallowed. "I don't suppose you could tell me what you think?" she asked hopefully.

For once, Prestwick didn't argue. "There's not much to tell. She was strangled with a stocking . . . her own, I presume, since I can see only one lying on top of her clothes here. It most likely happened early this morning. She put up a fight . . . there's blood under her nails. Probably gave the murderer a few nasty scratches before she died."

Cecily shivered. "There aren't that many guests staying at the hotel. I can't imagine one of them would have done this. If it had happened at the weekend I could have understood it more. We never know who might be playing in the card rooms . . . although the men who hire the rooms for the weekend are always quite reputable."

"The doubtful element is the people they bring in for the game," Prestwick said, wiping his hands on the towel. "After all, gambling isn't exclusively a gentleman's pursuit anymore. With the advent of the motorcar, more city dwellers have access to the seaside. You could well have some undesirable riffraff down there with stolen money to use for gambling.''

"It's possible, I suppose," Cecily murmured, feeling more than a little worried. The gambling rooms were hidden away in the wine cellars. The Pennyfoot's reputation for privacy and seclusion, as well as a tight-lipped staff, had made the card rooms a very large factor in the desirability of the hotel.

Although the constabulary were aware of the rooms, due to the fact that they were largely occupied by members of the aristocracy escaping the boredom of the city for a spot of spicy diversion, the police had turned a blind eye to their existence.

Now that the aristocracy were no longer coming down to the coast in large numbers, no doubt because of the influx of lower-class city dwellers, more and more the rooms were taken over by businessmen, entrepreneurs, stage people, and the like. As Prestwick said, Cecily had no real control over who might use the rooms.

As long as the card room was hired by a reputable guest for the weekend and paid for up front, he was free to bring in whom he liked to play the game. Now that Cecily really thought about it, the idea made her extremely uneasy.

"We have no card rooms open at present," she said abruptly, "and I'll see that they remain closed until we discover who is responsible for the death of this poor girl."

Prestwick gave her a look of approval. "What will your guests say if they have booked the card rooms and they find them closed?"

"They will simply have to understand. If there's any dissension, I'll return their money."

Prestwick nodded. "Bully for you," he murmured.

Neither one of them noticed Madeline, who had been standing quietly all this time, until she suddenly spoke, in the soft, eerie voice she always used when talking about things beyond the normal. "It's not the end," she said, staring straight ahead at the wall.

Cecily felt her skin creep. "What is it, Madeline?" she asked urgently.

Madeline pointed at the still, naked form in the bathtub. "I'm sorry, Cecily," she said, "but this is only the beginning. I can feel it all around me. There will be more before this is done."

Cecily stared at Prestwick, chilled by the disquiet in his face. Madeline had spoken with such conviction that this man, although steeped in scientific technology, looked utterly convinced of her disturbing words.

CHAPTER

❧ 4 ❧

"Do you think the police will catch the murderer, Miss Brown?" Emily asked timidly as she shoveled coal into the gaping mouth of the stove.

Gertie wiped the back of her hand across her sweating brow. " 'Course they will. They always do, don't they. 'Cept old Northcott will probably have to get some help from Madam and Mr. Baxter." Jutting her lower lip, she puffed air up her face. "He's bloody dense at times, our police constable. I sometimes wonder how he ever got to be a bl—bobby."

"Will they catch him soon?"

Gertie gave her a sharp look. "Well, you don't have nothing to worry about, do you. Mrs. Chubb says he'll be long gone by now."

Emily lifted the heavy coal bucket closer to the stove. Flames roared greedily as she threw a few more lumps into the smoldering furnace. "Well, he ain't gone, though, is he. I saw him. Me and Pansy both saw him."

Gertie started, almost dropping the pile of dishes she'd just taken down from the dresser. "You saw him? When? Where? Does Mrs. Chubb know?"

Emily shook her head, dislodging frail wisps of dark hair from under her cap. She hitched up her skirt to avoid dusting the hem with ashes as she leaned down to close the heavy door of the stove. "I just saw him a little while ago."

"Who did you see? Where was he? You're not bloody making this up, are you?"

Emily straightened, dabbing at her scarlet face with her sleeve. Her eyes looked wide and scared when she turned around. "I saw him when I was crossing the foyer. He stopped me and touched my arm with his bony fingers."

In spite of the heat from the stove, Gertie shuddered. "Go on. What did he say, then?"

"He said as how the world was coming to an end in a few days, and as how I ought to be prepared." Emily's lower lip quivered. "I don't know how to prepare for it, Miss Brown. I'm sc-scared."

Gertie wasn't feeling too confident herself right then. She wasn't about to let the little scullery maid see that, though. "Don't be a silly little twit, Emily. The world ain't coming to a bleeding end, is it. How can it, I mean? What's it going to do? Blow up? Not on your bleeding nelly, it ain't."

Emily sniffed. "You really think so?"

"I know so," Gertie said, managing to sound a good deal more assured than she felt.

"But what about the murderer? What if he kills someone else?"

"How'd you know it were the murderer? Did he tell you he did it?"

Emily shook her head.

"Did he try to strangle you?"

Emily shivered. "No, Miss Brown."

"Then you don't know," Gertie said and dumped the

plates on the tray with a decisive thud. "So take these bl—plates into the dining room and get them tables flipping laid before Mrs. Chubb gets back. Or the world might come to a flipping end for both of us."

"Yes, Miss Brown." Emily grunted as she picked up the heavy tray.

The door swung open just before she reached it, and Mrs. Chubb hurried in. Her face creased in dismay when she saw the tray on Emily's hands. "Those tables not laid yet? For heaven's sake, Emily, you'll have to move faster than that. We'll never get all this work done. Get a move on at once."

Emily uttered a squeak of protest and rushed out of the door.

"I don't know what we're going to do, that I don't," Mrs. Chubb muttered, crossing the red tile floor to the pantry. "If only Ethel hadn't had to go to that sanitarium, we might not be in the mess we are now."

"She's getting better, though, Mrs. Chubb." Gertie loaded a tray up with silverware, her hands flying as fast as she could manage. "I talked to Joe the other day, and he says as how the doctor told him she's not coughing as bad, and she's getting some of her weight back."

"Well, that is one piece of good news at least." The housekeeper disappeared into the pantry just as the door opened and two small children ran in.

"What're you doing in here?" Gertie demanded, staring down at her twins' grinning faces. Much as she loved to see them, their presence in the kitchen was usually a disaster.

"Mama!" Lillian tugged at Gertie's skirt, while James promptly sat down on the floor and pulled his mother's shoelace undone.

The door opened again, and Daisy rushed in, one hand on her chest as she gasped for breath. "I tell you, those two are faster than rabbits." She bent down and picked up a squirming James in her arms. "I was just on my way out to take them for a walk, but I had to show you this."

She shoved James under one arm, ignoring his howl of

protest as she dug into the pocket of her skirt and pulled out a crumpled letter. "It's from Doris. She's got a spot on the stage. It's only a small variety theater and it's only for one night. It's not even in London proper, it's on the outskirts, but Doris is real excited about it."

"What's this?" Mrs. Chubb came bustling out of the pantry, wiping her hands on her apron. "Our Doris is going to sing on the stage in London?"

Daisy nodded, her face flushed with pride. "Bella DelRay got her the job. She's the singer what stayed here last summer. Doris has been staying with her. Miss DelRay says as how there'd be more spots after Doris did this one, because she's so good."

"Well, I never." Mrs. Chubb took the proffered letter from Gertie's hand and scanned the neat scrawl.

Gertie felt a pang of envy and quickly squashed it. "She deserves it," she said stoutly. "Doris worked bloody hard to get there."

"She really did." Daisy took the letter back from Mrs. Chubb and shoved it in her pocket. "Now that Doris is definitely going to stay in London, I think I'll move up there, too. Doris says as how there's lots of jobs I can do . . . lots of nanny jobs. That's if you'll say a kind word for me, Miss Brown?"

Gertie stared at her in dismay. "But you can't bloody go to London. What about me babies? Who's going to take care of them?"

Daisy grabbed Lillian's hand and gave Gertie a worried look. "I'm sorry, Miss Brown, I really am. But Doris is my twin, and I want to be with her."

"Of course you do, Daisy." Mrs. Chubb shook her head. "Though what we shall do without you, heaven only knows. Does Madam know about this yet?"

Daisy shook her head. "I didn't like to tell her, what with all this fuss about the murder and all. I still feel faint when I think as how I found that poor girl dead like that. I expect Madam is still upset as well."

"Quite right." Mrs. Chubb glanced up at the clock. "I'll tell her later on. Now get those babies out of here before Michel gets back and starts throwing pans around again."

Gertie watched Daisy leave, carrying a wriggling twin under each arm. Cold fingers of dread crawled down her spine at the thought of Daisy leaving. How was she going to manage? She couldn't work with the babies constantly underfoot in the kitchen.

Apart from the fact that Mrs. Chubb wouldn't allow it, there were too many things the babies could get into and hurt themselves. Gertie picked up the tray of silverware and headed for the door. She couldn't afford another nanny, that was for sure. If it weren't for Daisy settling for half her pay, the babies wouldn't have a nanny now.

Out in the darkness of the hallway, she almost gave in to the tears threatening her. Just when things seemed to be going good for her, something always happened to mess it all up.

Immersed in her anxiety, she didn't see Samuel until she almost ran right into him.

"Here," he said sharply, "you'd better watch where you're going. Drop that lot and you'll cut someone's toes off."

"That ain't all I'd bleeding like to cut off," Gertie muttered darkly as she edged past him.

Samuel peered at her in the dim light from the gaslamps on the wall. "What's got you all gloom and doom? Not worried about that murderer, are you?"

"Wish that were all I had to worry about." Gertie heaved the tray higher on her stout hip.

"So what is it, then? The world coming to an end?" He grinned as if he'd made a great joke.

Gertie wasn't amused. She couldn't quite forget Emily's scared face when she'd talked about the strange man. "That ain't funny, Samuel. In any case, it's not got nothing to do with that. Daisy just told us she's leaving to go and live in London with Doris."

Samuel's expression changed at once to one of exaggerated innocence. "Oh, is she? Well, I'd better get off, then." He walked away, whistling softly as he shoved his thumbs into his waistcoat pockets.

Gertie stared after him for a minute. Samuel was up to something, that was for sure. He only whistled like that when he was into some mischief. She didn't have time to find out now, but she made up her mind right there and then that she'd find out what was going on before the day was out, or her name wasn't Gertie bloody Brown.

Cecily glanced at the grandfather clock as she reached the foot of the stairs. She'd promised Baxter she'd meet him in the roof garden, and already she was twenty minutes late. The most important appointment of her life was imminent, and she could very well miss it if she didn't hurry.

Although the surprise had been taken out of Baxter's proposal, the excitement was there just the same, and she couldn't wait to hear him utter again the words that she had longed to hear and had thought would never be spoken.

Baxter wanted her to marry him. Already her head swam with the hundred and one things she would have to do. Michael and Andrew would have to be told, of course, though she thought that it might not be too much of a surprise.

Although both her sons had met Baxter, neither of them really knew him. During the short time that Michael had owned the George and Dragon in Badgers End, he and Baxter had met on occasion, but Michael had never quite trusted him.

Cecily felt sure now that it was because Michael had perceived something that she had not until quite recently . . . that Baxter's high regard for her went much deeper than his professional status allowed.

Now she couldn't wait to hear him say the words once more, this time to cherish each syllable and commit them all to memory, so that in the years to come she could resurrect them in her mind a thousand times, and enjoy them as much as she would today. She might even be able to forget for a little while that another murder had been committed within the esteemed walls of the Pennyfoot Hotel.

Crackling with anticipation, she set her foot on the bottom step, just as a man approached her, calling her by name. At first she didn't recognize him, as he had his back to the front door which stood open, throwing him into silhouette.

But then she recognized his voice and was immediately wary. "Mr. Evans? What can I do for you?"

Sid Evans had arrived at the hotel yesterday, and she'd heard he was a motorcar salesman visiting Badgers End to evaluate the potential for a salesroom in the small town.

Personally Cecily didn't think that anyone in Badgers End could afford one of those monsters, except for Lord Withersgill perhaps. But then, he already owned two of them.

Sid Evans, however, seemed very sure of himself, and of his ability to sell motorcars in the village. He was a rather loud young man, and Cecily didn't care for his coarse attitude. Although his looks were pleasant enough, they were marred by some sort of skin disorder that caused his chin to look chafed and raw.

"Mrs. Sinclair," he said as he reached her. "I want to discuss a problem with you about my room."

Cecily winced, hating the way he put the emphasis on the first half of her surname, instead of the last, as anyone with any sense would know was the correct way to pronounce it. "Mr. Evans, I'm quite sure Mrs. Chubb would be happy to accommodate you. I trust the problem is not serious?" She couldn't help wondering if he'd heard about the murder, and his problem was somehow connected with that.

"Well, I do like to sleep nights, you know." His loud laugh rang out. "There's a very annoying tapping noise in my room all night. I think it's in the fireplace. I've taken a look up there, but I can't see anything."

"Oh, dear," Cecily murmured, trying to sound sympathetic. "I'll send Samuel up there to take a look."

"I don't think he's going to find anything. I'd say that

whatever gets in there at night disappears in the morning when it's daylight.''

"That could be." The clock chimed the half hour, and Cecily gave a guilty start. Baxter would think she'd forgotten about their rendezvous. "It was most likely an owl, Mr. Evans. I doubt very much if it will return. Now if you'll excuse me—''

"I don't care to stay there, Mrs. Sinclair. I want a room farther down the hall. There's one at the end of the corridor. I want that one.''

Cecily frowned. "I'll have to talk to Mr. Baxter about it, since he handles the reservations.''

Sid Evans let out a loud, long-suffering sigh. "And how long is that going to take, may I ask?''

"I'm meeting with him right now," Cecily said stiffly. "I'll send word to you this afternoon. Now, if you will please excuse me—''

"I want the one at the end of the corridor, mind you. It will be quieter there. Considering what I have to pay for a room in this establishment, I would expect at least some peace and quiet when I'm trying to sleep.''

Right then, she'd promise anything to be rid of the man. "Just move your things in there, Mr. Evans. I'll see that the new arrangements are taken care of, and I apologize for the inconvenience.''

"Not at all, Mrs. Sinclair." Now that he had his way, Sid Evans had apparently decided he could afford to be pleasant. "This is a nice hotel you have here. I'm looking forward to enjoying my stay at the Pennyfoot. I stayed in many a hotel during my acting days, but this is by far the nicest.''

"We shall enjoy having you," Cecily murmured insincerely.

Sid Evans looked as if he was about to answer, when he was interrupted by a high-pitched, breathless voice from across the foyer.

"Cecily, darling, there you are! I've been looking for you everywhere.''

Cecily groaned inwardly. Poor Baxter. He was not going to be happy with her. Turning to greet Phoebe, she returned the exquisitely dressed woman's effusive smile.

Phoebe always looked as if she'd just stepped down from a portrait. Her outfit today was outstanding. Her pale lilac gown swept about her ankles in a froth of white lace, and the high-buttoned lace collar was studded with seed pearls.

A wide band of purple velvet encircled Phoebe's delicate, nipped-in waist, and a row of pearls descended the full sleeves, ending in yet another band of lace at the wrists.

Phoebe's hat, as always, outshone the ensemble. Huge black ostrich feathers curled above purple petunias and pale green ribbon bows, while a white dove perched precariously on a sprig of silk laurel leaves.

Her delicate features nearly hidden by the enormous brim, Phoebe swept across the floor, one hand holding aloft a small package in a dramatic gesture, while the other clutched her parasol.

"My goodness, I'm quite out of breath," she declared as she came to a graceful halt beside Cecily. Her sharp gaze whisked over Sid Evans with a faint air of disapproval.

"I don't think you are acquainted with our guest," Cecily said, rather enjoying Phoebe's evaluation. "Mr. Evans, may I present Mrs. Phoebe Carter-Holmes, the mother of our local vicar and a very dear friend of mine."

"Mr. Evans sells motorcars," she added, turning to Phoebe.

As she had expected, Phoebe's face mirrored her contempt. She loathed the newfangled contraptions and anyone associated with them. Her expression changed to one of disgust, and she completely ignored the man's outstretched hand.

Instead, she looked him up and down and, in a voice loaded with contempt, muttered, "Really. How bizarre."

Sid Evans looked nonplussed. He withdrew his hand, nervously lifted it to adjust his tie, dropped his hand again, and said awkwardly, "If you ladies will excuse me?"

"Certainly," Cecily said serenely.

Phoebe refrained from answering at all.

After he'd made a rather hurried retreat, she sniffed. "Really, Cecily, the caliber of guests in this hotel is in a definite decline. You used to have such a select group of people staying here. Nowadays, just anyone is wandering in. How terribly depressing for you."

Cecily was inclined to agree, but she wasn't about to admit it out loud. "I'm sorry I had to cancel the committee meeting, Phoebe. Something urgent took my time away, I'm afraid."

"Oh, that's all right. Baxter was kind enough to bring me a tea tray. I must say, Cecily, Altheda Chubb's baking is fit for a king."

"And often has been," Cecily murmured.

"Anyway, I was hoping you could tell me where I could find Colonel Fortescue. It's his birthday today, you know. I thought I'd bring him a small present. Nothing very much, of course."

Intrigued, Cecily glanced at the neatly wrapped package. "I imagine he will be in the drawing room, enjoying his . . . newspaper." She had been going to say his usual tot of gin, but something in Phoebe's face stopped her.

In fact, Phoebe's face grew quite flushed as she nodded vigorously. "Well, in that case, I'll trot along and see if he's there. Thank you, Cecily. I'll just leave my parasol here, if you don't mind?"

"Not at all."

Phoebe deposited the white lace-trimmed parasol in the hallstand, then, with a wave of her hand, she tripped off down the hallway, leaving Cecily to wonder how Phoebe knew it was the colonel's birthday. In all the years he'd been visiting the hotel, as far as she knew he'd never mentioned it. It would seem as though Madeline was not the only one keeping secrets around the Pennyfoot.

Arriving breathlessly in the roof garden a few minutes later, Cecily was dismayed to find no one there. Baxter, it seemed, had given up on her. Now she would have to find him and apologize.

She made her way back down the stairs, rehearsing her speech. Unfortunately she was destined not to deliver it for a while. Pansy was waiting for her at the foot of the stairs and informed her that P.C. Northcott was waiting for Madam in the library.

Cecily changed direction, prepared for the worst.

CHAPTER

❧ 5 ❧

The constable was pacing impatiently back and forth when Cecily entered the quiet room. The library had always been one of her favorite places in the hotel. The rows of books lining the walls, the heavy oak paneling and marble fireplace, the long, dark Jacobean table, they were all so dear and familiar to her. She had spent many hours enjoying the restful ambience, and many a problem had been wrestled with inside these quiet walls.

At one time her late husband's portrait had graced the wall above the fireplace. She had taken it down several months ago, intending to replace it one day with a portrait of Baxter. She really must do that soon, Cecily thought, as she greeted the ruddy-faced constable.

"I see we have another h'unfortunate incident 'ere," the constable announced. He puffed out his chest, a habit that sorely threatened the buttons of his uniform. "I 'ave h'informed the inspector, and he will be along some time tomorrow. He is, at the moment, investigating a case in Wellercombe.''

As usual, Cecily thought darkly. Nevertheless, she was greatly relieved to learn that she had a day's grace before the inspector arrived.

"I have h'inspected the body," Northcott continued in his pompous voice, "and I 'ave the doctor's report. Having perused it, I shall now h'endeavor to remove the corpse and transport it to the station, until such time as how the doctor may make a more thorough investigation.''

Northcott always talked as if he were giving evidence in court. Normally Cecily tolerated the constable's annoying habits, but today she felt quite irritated with him.

"Well, I'm sure you will do whatever is necessary," she murmured. "Please let me know if I can offer any assistance. I do believe that Samuel is investigating a fireplace in one of the rooms, but he should be finished fairly shortly, if you should need a trap.''

"I would be much obliged, Mrs. Sinclair. I feel it is my duty to warn you that the murderer could still be at large in the 'otel. H'in which case, you and your staff, as well as your guests, could be in danger. I would suggest that everyone take extreme caution when dealing with strangers.''

"Of course, Constable. I'm sure my people will be careful.''

Northcott shook his head. "I never have enjoyed having to deal with a case like this. Just a child, she was. Makes you wonder what the world is coming to, doesn't it, when someone can be evil enough to take the life of a child.''

His concern seemed genuine enough, and Cecily relented. "What do you make of the shoe missing?" she asked, knowing full well she wouldn't get a satisfactory answer from the constable.

"As a matter of fact, Mrs. Sinclair, I haven't had time to ascertain that fact, as yet. She could have been wearing only one shoe at the time, you see. Until we h'establish that the shoe is not in her belongings, we cannot assume that it is missing.'' The constable cleared his throat, whipped out his notebook from the top pocket of his jacket, and dug in another pocket for a pencil.

Cecily tried not to grimace as he stuck out his tongue and licked the lead point. "Now,'' he said, "I would like your permission to question certain members of your staff, starting with yourself, if that is in order?''

She'd expected it, but even so it made her uneasy. Knowing she could hardly object without good reason, Cecily said carefully, "My staff are at your disposal, as always, Constable. I must, however, ask that you refrain from disturbing the guests unless absolutely necessary.''

"Yes, well, we'll have to see about that, won't we.'' Northcott scribbled something down in his notebook. "Now, when was the last time you saw Miss Flora Hatchett?''

Cecily frowned. "It was yesterday morning, when she arrived. I talked to all three new girls right here in the library before I sent them down to the kitchen with Gertie to meet Mrs. Chubb. They started work yesterday afternoon.''

"I see.'' The constable scribbled laboriously in his notebook. "What would Miss Hatchett have been doing in the bathroom at that early hour this morning?''

"Cleaning it, I presume,'' Cecily said, beginning to lose patience again. "Actually, Constable, I do believe Mrs. Chubb may be able to help you with these questions better than I can.''

"Yes, yes. Just one more, h'if I may?''

Cecily sighed. "Very well.''

"Did Miss Hatchett mention anything about a suitor, a secret admirer, or anything like that?''

Cecily looked at him in surprise. "Certainly not to me. But you might ask the other two new maids, Pansy and Emily. If anyone knows anything about that poor child—apart from her family, that is—it would be those two.''

"Yes, well, I understand you 'ave h'informed the girl's family.''

"This morning. Baxter gave them a ring on the telephone. They will be arriving in Badgers End this evening. Staying at the George and Dragon, I believe."

"Right. I'm sure they'll get in contact with me when they arrive."

"I did give them your name."

"Well, thank you, Mrs. Sinclair. That will be all for now. I'd like to search the girl's room, if I may?"

"Certainly." He wouldn't find anything there, she thought, since she'd already searched it and found nothing. Certainly not the missing shoe. She wasn't about to admit that to him, though.

She led him to the door, then paused with her hand on the handle. "Constable Northcott, as always, I can vouch for my staff without hesitation. I can assure you there isn't one amongst them who would be capable of a deed like this."

Northcott nodded. "That's as may be, Mrs. Sinclair. But we are all capable of murder. Every last one of us. I can't rule anyone out until I've satisfied myself that they have established their innocence."

She ushered him out of the door and closed it thankfully behind him. He was wasting his time questioning the staff. They were all intensely loyal, and even if they did know something, they would never pass it on to Northcott. She would have to question them all herself.

The door opened again, startling her. This time it was Samuel who entered the room, doffing his cap as he came. "I can't find nothing in that fireplace, mum," he said, standing respectfully by the door. "I can't see where any soot has been disturbed. I reckon whatever the gentleman heard, it ain't there no more."

"Well, I rather expected that." Cecily smiled. "Thank you, anyway, Samuel."

"Yes, mum." He hesitated, as if he wanted to say something, then apparently decided against it.

Intrigued, Cecily stopped him as he turned to leave. "Was there something else, Samuel?"

"Yes, mum. I mean, no, mum. I . . . was just going to say I could go up on the roof and look around the chimneys, if you like?"

Cecily studied him thoughtfully, wondering why she felt he was going to say something entirely different. "That might be a good idea, Samuel."

"Yes, mum."

Again he turned to leave, and again she stopped him. "Samuel, did you have a chance to talk to Flora Hatchett at all?"

"No, mum. I never spoke to her. I never met her."

Cecily nodded. "All right, Samuel. Thank you."

This time his hesitation was obvious. Concerned now, Cecily added quickly, "If you have something to tell me, Samuel, I do wish you would do so."

He looked down at his cap scrunched between his hands. "Well, mum, I don't know as if there's any truth to it, like, but I did hear Pansy talking about this man she saw."

Cecily narrowed her eyes. "What man? A guest, you mean?"

Samuel shrugged. "I don't think she really knows. Just said as how this bloke with a beard was wandering around the hotel and told her the world was coming to an end. Pansy said as how his eyes were really strange."

"I see," Cecily murmured, determining to have a word with Pansy at the earliest opportunity. "Well, thank you, Samuel, for bringing it to my attention."

"Yes, mum. Do you think we should search the hotel for the bloke?"

"I don't think that will be necessary, at least not yet. Have you mentioned this to anyone else?"

"No, mum." Samuel looked worried. "To tell the truth, I wasn't sure if Pansy was making the whole thing up. It's hard to tell when you don't know someone really well."

"In any case, under the circumstances, it might be better not to mention this to the constable. I'll have a word with Pansy myself."

"Yes, mum. Only Mrs. Chubb and Gertie heard Pansy talking about him, too."

"Well, we'll just have to hope they don't say anything either. At least until I've had a chance to hear Pansy's story."

"Yes, mum. I'll see that they get the message." Samuel flashed her a grin, then disappeared through the door.

Cecily took a moment to gather her thoughts. Was it possible a vagrant had wandered into the hotel and killed Flora? It didn't seem feasible, yet it could have happened.

Ever since she'd fired Ned for insulting the guests, Cecily had been looking for a new doorman. There just weren't that many men left in Badgers End either willing or capable of taking the job. With the door more or less unguarded during daylight hours, it was possible for anyone to walk into the hotel at will, without being noticed by the staff.

It certainly opened up a wide field of suspects, Cecily thought gloomily, as she prepared herself for her meeting with Baxter. If that was what had happened, things didn't bode well for the Pennyfoot's reputation, already badly tarnished by the spectacular disappearance of a magician's assistant from the hotel just a few weeks ago.

The girl had been found buried in the woods on Putney Downs, and since she was well known in the village, the case had caused quite a sensation.

Too much more of that, Cecily thought, hurrying down the hallway to Baxter's office, and Inspector Cranshaw would finally get his wish and close them down.

Gertie looked at the clock on the kitchen mantelpiece, amazed to see that the hands had barely moved. Ross's train had been due to arrive at the station twenty minutes ago. She'd seen Samuel leave to fetch him, and her stomach hadn't stopped rolling about ever since.

Now she couldn't concentrate on anything. Her hands felt sticky, her stomach hurt, and her head felt as if it had been stuffed with goosefeathers.

No matter how hard she tried, she couldn't stop looking at the clock, though that only seemed to make matters worse.

"Gertie!"

Mrs. Chubb's voice grated in her ear, and she jumped. "Bloody hell. You'll make me die of fright, you will."

"For heaven's sake, girl. Why don't you just go upstairs and wait for him in the foyer?"

Gertie felt her face growing warm. She reached for the aluminum milk jug and mumbled, "I don't know what you mean."

"Of course you know what I mean." The housekeeper took the jug from her hands. "I'll fill that. The way you're going on you'll spill the milk all over the floor."

"I've got to do something. I might as well fill the bleeding milk jug."

"Go on upstairs and do what you're told. You're no good to me like this."

Mrs. Chubb gave her a little push, and Gertie obediently headed for the door. She looked back as she reached it and gave the housekeeper a shaky grin. "Ta, Mrs. Chubb. I'll be back as soon as I've spoken to him. I promise."

"You'd better be back by half past three, my girl. Someone has to make the lobster salad, and I don't have time to do it."

"I'll be back." Excitement took her breath away, and she rushed out of the door, eager now to see the man who had occupied so much of her thoughts the past few weeks.

She had dreamed of their reunion for so long, imagining how it would be. They would see each other at the same time, rush toward each other and embrace. She still remembered what she'd felt like when Ross had kissed her. She couldn't wait to feel like that again.

She paused at the top of the kitchen stairs and straightened her cap, tucking in the stray wisps of her dark hair. With shaking fingers, she shoved her apron strap back onto her shoulder and inspected her skirts to make sure they weren't dusted in flour.

Her shoes could have done with a shine, but it was too late now. Through the open door she could see the trap pulling up in front of the white stone steps of the hotel.

Her heart was thumping so hard she felt faint. She'd read about women swooning when they'd met someone they really cared about. Somehow she couldn't see herself sinking gracefully to the floor with one delicate hand pressed to her brow. Ross would probably bleeding laugh at her. He was always teasing her.

A man climbed down from the trap, and she stopped breathing. She couldn't see his face, but she'd have known that tall, stocky build and thick, dark hair anywhere.

Her fingers plucked nervously at her skirt as she waited, and for one ridiculous moment she thought about running away. Then his tall figure filled the doorway, and she made a little sound in her throat. Now she couldn't move if the devil himself was facing her.

"Well, well," Ross McBride said in his deep, Scottish brogue, "if it isn't the fairest lass I ever set eyes upon. How are ye, Gertie?"

She had never had trouble talking to men in her entire life, but right then she couldn't seem to speak at all. Making a great effort to sound normal, she said gruffly, "I'm very well, thank you. It's truly nice to see you again, Ross."

He came forward, followed by Samuel dragging a large trunk behind him. Gertie watched him approach, wondering frantically what he intended to do. He could hardly kiss her right in front of Samuel. That wouldn't be proper. Not that she'd mind it, of course.

"I'll take this along to your room, Ross," Samuel said cheerfully. "It's at the end of the hallway. Gertie can show you where it is, can't you, love." To Gertie's dismay, he gave her a slow, lascivious wink.

Praying that Ross hadn't noticed, she scowled at him. "Get along with you, Samuel. Mr. Baxter's looking for you."

Samuel's chuckle seemed to echo across the foyer long

after he'd disappeared. Gertie looked up at Ross, wondering how she could have forgotten the way his hazel eyes twinkled when he looked at her.

"You look thinner, lass. Have ye no' been eating right?"

"I eat just fine." She managed to work her mouth into a smile. "You look just the bl—same as you did when you left."

His hearty laugh rang out, warming her whole body. "I reckon I got a few more gray hairs since I last saw you. How are the wee bairns?"

"Not so wee anymore." She held out her hand, palm down. "This big now."

"Go on with you, I dinna believe it." Ross shook his head. "I brought them each a wee kilt. I just hope they fit them now."

"I'll make them fit." That's what was different about him, Gertie realized. He wasn't wearing his kilt. The last time she'd seen him he'd been staying at the hotel while he took part in a bagpipe competition. He was the only one out of all the pipers she saw who looked masculine in a kilt. She'd never seen him in trousers before. He looked taller somehow, and older than she remembered. A feeling of panic welled up, and she almost choked on it.

"I brought a wee gift for you, too, lass. I'll give it to you when I unpack."

"I have something for you, too. It's in my room." She colored, hoping he didn't think she was making an improper suggestion. "I'll fetch it later. Right now I s'pose you should report to Mr. Baxter. He's probably in his office."

Ross nodded gravely. "I suppose I should. Would ye care to show me the way, then?"

She nodded, dropping her gaze. She felt awkward and bitterly disappointed. This wasn't the way she'd imagined it at all. It was as if they'd just met, and none of the tender things they'd said to each other in their letters ever existed.

Ross was certainly friendly, but she could tell he was being very careful what he said. He hadn't made an attempt to touch her, just stood looking down at her as if he wasn't sure what he wanted to say next. She wasn't at all sure she wanted him to touch her now.

Perhaps now that he'd seen her again, he'd changed his mind about his feelings for her. She couldn't really blame him if he did. After all, she had told him she couldn't marry him and go to Scotland with him.

She'd missed him so dreadfully, but now that he was here, this big, burly Scotsman with his laughing eyes and his kind, teasing voice seemed like a stranger.

"It's right down here," she said, trying not to let him see how upset she was. With her head held high and her back stiff, she marched down the hallway to Mr. Baxter's office.

The manager answered her light tap with a curt, "Come in!"

Gertie opened the door and stuck her head in. "Mr. McBride is here," she said, then, catching sight of Madam seated in front of the desk, added hurriedly, "if this is a good time, mum?"

"A perfect time," Cecily said, rising from her chair. "I'm anxious to see Mr. McBride again."

Gertie opened the door wider to let Ross pass.

"Come in, come in," Baxter said, coming forward to greet the Scotsman. "Welcome to the Pennyfoot Hotel."

Ross winked at Gertie, setting off her stomach again. "I'll be seeing you later," he whispered, then stepped inside the office to shake Baxter's outstretched hand.

Gertie left him there, trying hard not to feel so let down. After all, he'd just arrived, after a long trip from Scotland. He was probably tired. Things would be better when he'd had a chance to rest, and she'd become more used to seeing him again.

She had to keep repeating those words to reassure herself as she made her way slowly back to the kitchen.

CHAPTER

🎗 6 🎗

"Now, what is it you wanted to say to me before we were interrupted?" Baxter asked after Ross had left the office.

Cecily squirmed on her chair. She could tell he was upset and could hardly blame him. She had failed him, and he had every right to be annoyed with her. What she didn't need now was more disagreement. Already the twinges of a headache were making themselves felt.

"What did you think of Ross McBride as our new gardener?" she countered, hoping to delay the inevitable argument.

"I think he is an excellent choice and will handle things very well, considering he is not a professional gardener. He seems to be well enough informed, which is really all the job requires. As well as a willingness to work hard, of course."

"I agree. Although I'm quite sure Gertie suggested him

for personal reasons, for once things turned out well for all of us.''

"I was under the impression that you did not come here to discuss Mr. McBride's qualifications."

The cold glint in Baxter's gray eyes warned her that his patience was wearing thin. Giving up her attempt to postpone matters, she lifted her chin. "I did not. I came here to apologize for keeping you waiting in the roof garden. I was unavoidably delayed."

"So I assume. An unfortunate state of affairs that is becoming annoyingly frequent of late."

"I'm sorry, Bax. I know this meeting was important to you—"

"And to you, I'd hoped."

"Well, of course it was, and under any other circumstances I would have been there. You know I would. It's just that this murder business has created even more problems, and I'm doing my best to keep the news quiet from the guests and—"

"Cecily." Baxter's voice was quiet but effective. "Are you aware the business of this hotel is seriously disrupting our courtship?"

She felt suddenly breathless. "Yes, of course. I'm sorry, Baxter, I really am, but I don't see what else we can do. At least until the season is over. We need the money, as you well know. As long as we have guests, there will be business to worry about. We can hardly run the hotel without it."

"I am aware of that." He looked quite grim for a moment, tapping the quill of his pen against the ink well. "I suppose we must find a new maid to replace Flora as soon as possible." His face softened. "It's not entirely your fault. I understand that the hotel business must come first, but at times it can be extremely vexing."

"I know, Baxter, I know." Cecily sighed. "To be honest, the way things are going here, we might not have to worry about it much longer. Inspector Cranshaw is losing patience with the problems we have had here, and I'm afraid that this latest episode might just be the last straw."

Baxter threw down his pen and leaned back in his chair. "The problem, of course, lies in the card rooms. Our more affluent guests from London are now taking their holidays abroad. We are seeing an entirely different kind of visitor to Badgers End. Some of those people I've come across when passing through the cellars make me shudder."

Cecily stroked her fingers across her aching brow. "I know what you mean. Though I really don't know what we should do about it."

"There's only one thing we can do about it." He leaned forward, his gaze hard on her face. "We must close the card rooms down, Cecily. The sooner the better. Today, preferably. Before Cranshaw has the chance to use them as an excuse to close the Pennyfoot."

She gazed back at him, perilously close to shedding a tear. "I had already decided to close them down temporarily. I suppose it's just a matter of not opening them up again."

His face was full of sympathy, though she could see the relief in his eyes. "I think that is a very wise decision."

"Oh, Baxter." Her sigh seemed to hang in the air between them. "How will we manage without them? The card rooms are the reason most of our guests spend so much time at the Pennyfoot. Without them, we shall be no better than any other hotel. Less, in fact, since we are lacking many of the modern amenities now offered by the better hotels in Wellercombe."

"We shall simply have to find another reason for guests to enjoy the Pennyfoot. More select guests than those who frequent the card rooms."

She stared at him, helpless to explain the depression she felt. "Baxter," she said at last, "I'm afraid. For the first time, I'm truly afraid."

He rose swiftly, skirting the desk to reach her side. His arms felt comforting as they closed around her. "My dear madam," he said softly, "there is no need to feel afraid when I am here to protect you and care for you. One thing I must ask of you, however.''

Although she felt certain she knew what he would ask, she waited, wondering how she could possibly answer him.

''I must beg you to promise me faithfully that you will not become involved in this police investigation. In view of the fact that you narrowly escaped with your life a few weeks ago, I cannot allow you to take such risks again.''

She felt too dispirited to argue over what he was entitled to allow, as she normally would. Instead, she lifted her hands and let them drop again. Leaning against him, she said quietly, ''How can I turn my back on everyone and allow the hotel to sink into oblivion, as it will surely do unless I attempt to solve this before the inspector decides to close us down?''

''I would rather we lose the hotel than lose you.'' He bowed his head, resting his chin on her forehead. ''I can manage without the Pennyfoot. We both can. I really don't think I could survive without your wonderful smile and your spirited, though sometimes illogical, comments.''

She had to smile at that. ''Someone has to keep you on your toes.''

''And you do an admirable job, my dear madam.''

''Did I ever tell you, Bax, that you are the light of my life?''

He dropped a swift kiss on her forehead. ''You are the soul of mine.''

The double rap on the door drew them apart. Baxter paused a moment, as if to collect his thoughts, then called out brusquely, ''Yes?''

''It's Samuel, sir. Gertie said you were looking for me?''

''Ah, yes. I'll be there in a moment.'' He held out his hand, and Cecily took it, allowing him to draw her to her feet. ''Please, Cecily, heed my warning. You have come too close to danger too many times. Sooner or later your luck will run out. I could not bear it if anything happened to you now.''

She touched his cheek with her fingers. "Dear Baxter, I shall be careful, I promise."

He nodded, though he looked unconvinced. "Shall we reschedule our tryst?"

She smiled. "This evening, perhaps?"

"Perfect. The cocktail hour. I should be able to get away then."

"I'll meet you in the roof garden."

"Until then." His look warmed her, as the sun on the hottest day could never do.

He escorted her to the door and opened it for her. She smiled at Samuel as she stepped past him in the hallway, and rather enjoyed the stable manager's look of speculation.

No doubt soon the entire hotel staff would know of her true relationship with Baxter, if they hadn't guessed it already. She could say nothing, however, until Baxter had repeated his proposal and she had formally accepted.

This evening, she promised herself as she hurried along the hallway. And this time she would allow nothing to spoil the occasion.

Gertie grunted as she carried the loaded tray of soiled dishes to the kitchen. They seemed to get heavier each time she carried them, yet there had been only a few guests in the dining room for the midday meal. The trouble was, Pansy was trying to pile everything onto one tray, in order to save time.

It was all bloody right for Pansy, Gertie thought as she heaved the tray higher up her hip. Pansy didn't have to carry the bleeding things.

She rounded the corner, screeching to a quick halt as a man loomed up ahead of her. "Please excuse me, sir," she muttered, lowering her chin as she attempted to pass him.

"Wait a minute, my pretty. What's your hurry?"

Gertie peeped up at him warily. She knew his type. Thought they was bleeding God's gift to women, they did. She'd already been warned about Sid Evans but hadn't paid much attention at the time. The men didn't usually make advances to her. She was too tall, too big, too clumsy, too flipping unladylike. The men usually went for girls like Pansy and Emily, who went in and out where they was supposed to.

Looking up into Sid Evans's grinning face, however, she began to feel just a little uneasy. She didn't want to be rude to a guest, especially since there weren't that many of them anymore, but she weren't going to take no guff off this bloke, no matter what.

"Excuse me, sir," she said again, with just a slight edge to her voice. "I have to take these dishes back to the kitchen. And they're heavy."

"I'm sure a big, strapping girl like you can manage just fine."

Gertie bit back her resentment. He was a guest, and she had to be polite. "Yes, sir. Now, if you'll just let me pass."

"There's room for you to get by." He leered at her. "I don't mind a bit of tit in my face."

Gertie forgot all about him being a guest. She lifted the tray above her head. "What you'll get, you saucy bugger, is my bloody fist in your mouth if you don't flipping move. Now sod off, before I drop this bleeding lot on your head."

Sid Evans clutched his chest. "How wonderful! She loves me. I am indeed a lucky man."

"Drop dead," Gertie said rudely and shoved past him, almost sending him into the wall. His laugh followed her all the way down the steps to the kitchen.

When she pushed the door open with her knee, however, she soon forgot about Sid Evans and his crude remarks. Emily was there, in tears, with Mrs. Chubb's arm around her frail shoulders.

"There, there, child," the housekeeper murmured, giving Gertie a warning look.

Gertie knew what that look meant. Not that she was in any mood to make fun of the girl in any case. "What's up with her?'' she demanded as she dropped the tray with a crash on the table.

At the sound of it, Emily let out a shriek and cried harder.

Mrs. Chubb frowned. "She's been frightened by one of the guests. And that didn't help."

"Beg your bloody pardon." Gertie narrowed her eyes. "Who scared her, then? Wasn't that creepy bugger, Sid Evans, was it? I just met him in the hallway. Sent him off with a bleeding flea in his ear, I did."

The housekeeper uttered a shocked gasp. "You did what? You weren't rude to a guest, I hope?"

"He was bloody rude to me first." Gertie picked up a pile of plates from the tray and took them over to the sink.

"Gertie Brown. You know very well that no matter what a guest might say, you are supposed to hold your tongue and mind your manners. If the maids show no respect, no wonder we are losing guests."

Gertie dumped the plates into the hot, foamy water and spun around. "And what about respect to me? Why do I have to keep me bleeding mouth shut when a dirty rotter like Sid Evans says nasty things to me?"

Mrs. Chubb's expression hardened. "Because that's the way things are, and well you know it. I didn't make up the rules. Anyway, it wasn't Sid Evans who frightened Emily."

"Who was it, then?"

Emily, who had quietened down, burst into tears again.

"Come, come, Emily," the housekeeper said with a trace of impatience in her voice. "The man is just teasing you, that's all. The world is not coming to an end, nor will it ever, so hush with that noise and blow your nose. You look quite a sight with all those tears on your face."

Emily pulled a square of linen from the pocket of her apron and dabbed at her face.

"Oh, him again?" Gertie came back to the table for more dishes. "Who is he, then?"

Mrs. Chubb looked worried. "Nobody seems to know.

Samuel told Madam about him, but she didn't seem to know who he was, either.''

"Sounds like one of them gypsies wandering around if you ask me.''

"He didn't look like no gypsy,'' Emily said timidly. "His clothes were too good for that. And his hands were all white and smooth. Not rough and dirty like a gypsy's hands.''

"Well, whoever he is, take no notice of him,'' Mrs. Chubb said briskly. "Now get started on those dishes, Emily, before Michel comes in and starts complaining.''

"Michel's always bleeding complaining,'' Gertie muttered. "He ain't bloody happy unless he's complaining.''

"You haven't told me about your meeting with Ross McBride yet,'' Mrs. Chubb said, deftly changing the subject.

Gertie dried her hands on her apron. "That's because there ain't nothing to tell. I said hello, then I took him down to Mr. Baxter's office. I haven't seen him since.''

"How did he look?''

Gertie shrugged. "Same as always.''

Mrs. Chubb gave her a sharp look, but much to Gertie's relief, she said no more on the subject. Gertie was glad about that. She wouldn't want Mrs. Chubb to know that she'd been stupid enough to imagine a romantic reunion with Ross McBride, and he'd acted as if she were nothing more than a flipping housemaid. Which, of course, she was. The thought depressed her to no end.

CHAPTER

❀ 7 ❀

Phoebe heard Colonel Fortescue's gruff voice while she was still halfway down the hallway. She had just about given up any chance of finding him. When she'd found the drawing room empty, she had gone in search of him in the gardens. It had taken her quite a while to satisfy herself that the colonel was not enjoying the warm sunshine, and had been on her way back to the hotel when she'd encountered the Pennyfoot's new gardener.

She remembered Ross McBride fondly from his last visit to the hotel, and was delighted to discover that he would be working at the Pennyfoot. After a brief conversation with him, she had returned to the hotel, and was on her way to find Cecily when she'd heard the colonel in the drawing room.

He appeared to be talking to someone, though that wasn't

by any means certain, since the colonel talked quite vigorously to himself at times.

When she heard a deep voice answering him, however, Phoebe hesitated before entering the drawing room. As eager as she was to present the colonel with his birthday present, since she was tired of carrying it around with her, she had no wish to do so in front of someone else.

While she was still dithering, however, Samuel passed her in the hallway. "Good day to you, Mrs. Carter-Holmes," he said in his cheerful voice. "How's the vicar, then? I trust he is well?"

"Algie is very well, thank you, Samuel."

"I'm glad to hear it."

Phoebe watched the stable manager walk jauntily away. He seemed in remarkably good spirits, she thought, listening to him whistling a catchy tune. Quite a change from his dark moods recently. Ever since that funny little maid, Doris, had left, in fact.

The door to the drawing room, which had stood ajar, abruptly opened. "There you are, old bean. Thought I heard your ravishing voice."

Phoebe hid the package behind her back as she surveyed the colonel. "I thought I'd drop by to wish you a happy birthday, Colonel, but since you are engaged—"

"No, no, old girl. Come on in. I want you to meet this chappie."

He stood back, allowing her to enter.

Phoebe walked into the room and stopped dead. For a minute she thought she was seeing double. "Great heavens," she exclaimed, staring at the man who had risen to his feet.

"Madam?" The gentleman inclined his head.

"Oh, yes, well . . ." Fortescue stuttered. "This is the lady I was telling you about, old chap. Phoebe Carter-Holmes. Phoebe, my dear, I'd like you to meet Brigadier Albert Chatsworth, Her Majesty's Army Corps."

"Retired," the brigadier corrected. "And it's His Majesty's army now.'' He clicked his heels smartly and raised Phoebe's hand to his lips. ''At your service, madam. Colonel Fortescue mentioned that you were an enchanting creature, but he failed to describe your dazzling beauty.''

Totally charmed, Phoebe gazed up at the white-whiskered face of the brigadier. Now that she had taken a closer look, she could see the difference between the two men. Brigadier Chatsworth's eyes were brown, whereas Colonel Fortescue's eyes were a light shade of blue. And tinged with red more often than not.

The brigadier's nose was straight and thin, unlike the colonel's rather bulbous, heavily veined proboscis. In fact, although at first glance the two men appeared to be identical, there was no doubt the brigadier was by far the more handsome of the two.

Feeling somewhat flustered, Phoebe took back her hand. ''Delighted to meet you, Brigadier. A pleasure, I'm sure.''

''The pleasure is all mine, madam. It isn't often one meets such a vision of elegance and grace. Colonel Fortescue is a fortunate man indeed.''

Phoebe glanced at the colonel, who seemed to have turned an odd shade of purple. She couldn't imagine what the old fool had been telling this fascinating man, but she was quite sure she wouldn't care for it.

She could only hope that Colonel Fortescue hadn't had the extreme bad taste as to recount the incident in the rose garden, when she had mistakenly taken a few drops of brandy, strictly for medicinal purposes of course, and had become rather light-headed as a result.

''I haven't the slightest idea to what you could be referring,'' she said primly. ''The colonel and I are mere acquaintances, that is all.''

The colonel looked most distressed. ''I say, old bean, that's not exactly cricket, you know.''

Ignoring him, she bestowed her smile on the imposing brigadier. ''You are staying at the Pennyfoot long?''

"Just until the weekend. Came down for a spot of fresh sea air, what?"

Good heavens, Phoebe thought. He even talked like the colonel. "I trust your wife is enjoying her stay?"

The brigadier uttered a deep chuckle that seemed to shiver all over her. "Not married, madam. Just a happy bachelor, that's me."

"Really," Phoebe murmured. "How utterly fascinating."

Fortescue cleared his throat, a little too loudly. "I say, Phoebe, is that for me?"

She'd forgotten about the package clutched in her hand. More reluctant than ever to admit she had brought him a present, she looked down at it as if she'd never seen it before. While she was still trying to think of a way to explain the package, the colonel took hold of her arm with a proprietary gesture that quite irritated her.

"If you'll excuse us, old boy, I'd like to have a word with the lady in private."

She opened her mouth to protest, but the brigadier forestalled her.

"Not at all, old man. Got to run along myself, in any case. Pleasure to meet you, Mrs. Carter-Holmes. I sincerely hope we shall meet again before I return to the city."

Phoebe batted her eyelids at him. "I certainly hope so, Brigadier," she said breathlessly.

"Come on, old girl, there's something I want to tell you." The colonel gave an annoying tug on her arm, and she turned on him, pulling her elbow sharply from his grasp. "Really, Colonel!"

"Sorry, old girl. But I'm anxious to say this before I forget what I was going to say. Dashed memory isn't what it used to be, you know."

Phoebe suspected that the colonel was far more interested in removing her from the brigadier's scintillating presence than in any story he might have to tell, but she refrained from saying so.

With a final bow in her direction, the gentleman left the

drawing room, and she was left alone to deal with the visibly agitated colonel.

"Well, what is it?" she demanded, a trifle waspishly.

The colonel puffed and blew as if he'd been running a great distance. His eyelids flapped up and down so fast his eyes looked blurry. "Not here, old girl. Out in the blasted rose garden."

"But I've just come from there. It's rather too warm to keep walking to and fro through the gardens." She didn't add that she'd been looking for him for some time. She couldn't think now why she'd wasted so much time trying to find him, when there were captivating gentlemen like the brigadier in the vicinity.

"Madam, I implore you. It's blasted important."

"Oh, very well." She might as well find out what the silly man wanted to tell her. Now that her curiosity was aroused, she would do well to satisfy it. In any case, she really didn't need to carry the package around much longer. She should give it to him and be done with it.

Deciding to wait until they had reached the rose garden, she trotted alongside the colonel as he marched purposefully, if somewhat unsteadily, out to the gardens.

The roses were in full bloom, and the fragrance seemed overpowering as they entered through the arbor. Phoebe was relieved to see that the garden was deserted. She had no wish for the world to see her give the colonel a present. In fact, now that she had time to review the situation, she was beginning to wish she'd never considered it in the first place.

She'd felt sorry for the colonel, since he always seemed so alone, and people for the most part kept out of his way. When she'd learned of his upcoming birthday, she'd crocheted a nightcap to keep his head warm on cold winter nights.

Now that she thought about it, the present seemed a little too personal. A bottle of Tanqueray gin would have been a more apt choice, she thought darkly.

Nevertheless, she seated herself on the bench and thrust

the package at him. "This is a small gift for your birthday. I do hope it fits."

The colonel took the package from her as if he were handling the most precious treasure in the world. "For me? Oh, I say, old bean. Jolly thoughtful of you, what? What is it?"

"Well, open it, and then you'll see." She glanced around, assuring herself that no one was watching them.

Fortescue fumbled with the wrapping for so long she was ready to scream. Finally he withdrew the cap and held it up. After a moment's silence, during which Phoebe cursed herself for her stupidity, he said in a voice filled with reverence, "Madam, this is the most beautiful thing that anyone has ever done for me. I shall treasure it always."

For a moment she was quite touched, then to her dismay, the colonel pulled the cap on and stuck his head to one side at a jaunty angle. "How does it look?"

Horrified, she cast a hunted look around. "For heaven's sake, Colonel, take it off at once. Do you want everyone to see it?"

He seemed not to hear her. For a long moment he stared down at her, then to her utter astonishment, he got down rather unsteadily on one knee.

Fearing that he was about to embark on one of his strange fits, Phoebe drew away from him in alarm. "Colonel, what on earth do you think you are doing?"

He reached for her hand, but she managed to elude his grasp. Thoroughly unsettled now, she made to get up, but he was directly in front of her, and she couldn't move without pushing him away and possibly endangering them both.

"Phoebe, my dear," he began in a voice quite unlike his own, "I must ask you to listen, as I have something of great importance to say to you."

She must humor him. Maybe the fit would pass, or perhaps Mr. McBride would appear and save her. It was too much to expect Brigadier Chatsworth might charge to her rescue, but one could always hope. "Very well, Colonel," she said briskly. "But do hurry up and get on with it. This sun is really quite warm." To emphasize her point, she withdrew her lace handkerchief and delicately fanned her face.

"I have admired you from a distance for a long time," Fortescue said, stumbling over the words. "It is only recently, however, that you have given me enough encouragement to permit me to hope that you would greatly honor me with your hand in marriage."

Stunned beyond belief, Phoebe could only stare at him. It wasn't as if she hadn't entertained the idea. It had occurred to her some time ago that the colonel was well able to keep her in the custom with which she was once acquainted. That was before her dear departed Sedgely's upper-crust family disowned both her and her son, Sedgeley's rightful heir, who was but a child at the time.

The colonel had seemed to be a solution to her present predicament, which bordered on poverty and to which she would never become accustomed. After meeting Brigadier Chatsworth today, however, and receiving such effusive praise and admiration, she had been visibly reminded that the colonel wasn't necessarily the only tadpole in the pond, so to speak.

Of course, the fool had to wait until now to ask for her hand, just when she was beginning to enjoy the attentions of another man. That was so typical of Colonel Fortescue.

Searching for a way to let him down lightly, she played for time. "I beg your pardon?"

"I know this is sudden, my dear, but it is nonetheless sincere. I am asking you to be my wife."

Well, it was rather flattering, she supposed. No matter how strange the man was, he had been very attentive of late. "This is a great surprise, colonel," she murmured, keeping her eyes downcast. "I must ask you for time to consider your gracious proposal."

"Then you do care for me?"

He looked so anxious and quite endearing for a change. Relenting, she patted his hand. The poor man badly needed a woman to take care of him. If it had been at any other time, she might well have considered his proposal. "Of course I care for you, Colonel. I shall give you your answer in a day or two." Thereby giving herself enough time to formulate a proper response. Maybe Algie could help. He was rather good at putting things into words.

"I say, old bean, do you think you could manage to call me by my Christian name? It's Frederick, you know. Bit of a blasted mouthful, I suppose. You could shorten it to Fred if you prefer."

Phoebe shuddered. "I think I prefer Frederick, Colonel."

He looked so deliriously happy as she helped him to his feet that she felt a stab of remorse. She would have to use the utmost diplomacy when giving him her refusal. The last thing she wanted to do was hurt his feelings. One never knew with the colonel when he was going to do himself or someone else bodily harm.

Cecily was forced to wait until late afternoon to question Pansy. She found her, as she expected, alone in the dining room, setting up the tables for the evening meal. The maid seemed startled to see her and dropped a deep curtsey.

"I won't keep you long, Pansy," Cecily said, trying to relax the child with a smile. "I simply wanted to know if things are going well for you here at the Pennyfoot."

"Oh, yes, mum," Pansy assured her, nodding vigorously. "I'm ever so happy here, mum."

"I'm pleased to hear that. If you do have any problems with your job, the staff, or with any of the guests, please inform either me or Mrs. Chubb, and we shall endeavor to straighten out the matter."

"Yes, mum. Thank you, mum."

Cecily waited, but when it became apparent that Pansy had nothing further to say, she prompted her gently. "Samuel tells me you encountered a rather strange man in the hallways."

"Yes, mum. At least, I think he was strange. He kept telling me the world was coming to an end."

"I see." Cecily frowned. "Did he say anything else?"

"Just to be prepared for *the end*." She'd pronounced the last two words in a deep voice, sweeping the room in a dramatic gesture.

"Did you recognize him as one of the guests?"

"No, mum. I never saw him before. But then, I haven't seen all the guests, neither."

"What did he look like?"

"Sort of short like . . . and he had a beard. And weird eyes, like he was looking right through you. Gave me the shivers, he did."

"You don't know what room he's supposed to be in?"

"No, mum, he didn't say."

"Well, when you see him again, please ask him. If he doesn't belong in the hotel, I'll have the police look into it."

"Yes, mum." She chewed on her lip for a moment. "You don't think he's the murderer, do you? Emily saw him again this afternoon, and he frightened her with his talk about the end of the world."

Knowing how fertile young girls' imaginations can be, Cecily thought it far more likely that the maids were simply over-reacting to one of the guests, many of whom were inclined to be just a tad eccentric. "I really don't think he would be walking around the hotel after committing such a crime. Nevertheless, you should always take care when talking to a stranger, no matter where you are."

"Yes, mum."

Cecily hesitated. "Where is Emily now? In the kitchen?"

"Yes, mum. She was washing dishes when I left."

"I'll have a quick word with her as well, then." Cecily did her best to give the girl a smile. "Thank you, Pansy. And keep up the good work. Mrs. Chubb is very pleased with you."

The maid's face flushed with pleasure. "Yes, mum. Thank you, mum."

Nice little thing, Cecily thought as she left the dining room and headed for the kitchen. It was so difficult to find efficient staff nowadays; it was a joy to find someone willing to work, and who actually appeared to enjoy it.

She reached the kitchen, to find utter chaos. Michel was in one of his moods apparently, as he banged and crashed the heavy metal pots around with gusto.

Gertie stood in the middle of the floor arguing with Mrs. Chubb, her cap on sideways, as usual, her face flushed with temper.

Mrs. Chubb caught sight of Cecily first and gave Gertie a warning nudge in the side, while Samuel leaned against the sink, looking as if he was thoroughly enjoying the racket.

Gertie swore and glanced over her shoulder, then immediately dropped a curtsey when she saw Cecily standing there. "Sorry, mum. Didn't see you come in."

"I'm not surprised," Cecily said mildly. She looked at the flustered housekeeper. "Whatever is the matter, Mrs. Chubb? I could hear your voices all the way down the hall."

Mrs. Chubb wrung her hands in the folds of her apron. "I'm so sorry, madam. I'm afraid tempers are a little short down here, on account of the shortage of help, you see."

Cecily sighed. "Yes, I do sympathize with you all. I do understand that Flora's death is not only quite upsetting, but it has also put an extra burden on the staff. I must remind you all, however, that we still have a hotel to run, and guests who expect the same excellent service we have always provided at the Pennyfoot. Mr. Baxter and I will do our best to remedy the situation as soon as possible."

"Yes, mum. Thank you, mum. It's just that Emily is missing now, and the tables have to be laid and salads to be made. I was just asking Gertie to go down to the wine cellar—"

"Wine cellar?" Cecily didn't like the sharp pang of uneasiness she felt at the housekeeper's words.

"Yes, mum. I sent Emily down there to fetch some wine at least half an hour ago. She's inclined to dawdle, mum, that's the problem."

"I'll go and bleeding hurry her up," Gertie muttered,

heading for the door. "Strewth, I don't have time to do me own work, leave alone everyone else's."

"Gertie, that's enough of that bad language," Mrs. Chubb rapped out. "Remember to whom you are talking, please."

Gertie gave Cecily a guilty glance. "Sorry, mum."

Cecily paid her no attention. She was too busy wondering just why Emily had been delayed for so long in the wine cellar.

CHAPTER
❀ 8 ❀

Cecily glanced at the grandfather clock in the foyer as she crossed to the stairs. The Westminster chimes softly announced the half hour, meaning she was due in the roof garden to meet with Baxter.

She couldn't help wishing that he had chosen another time to ask for her hand in marriage. It was a little difficult to concentrate on her own happiness when there was so much trouble in the hotel.

She reached the stairs and set her foot on the bottom step. Before she could mount them, however, a tall, distinguished-looking gentleman stepped out of the shadows in the hallway and addressed her by name.

"Mrs. Sinclair, I have been looking forward to meeting with you."

She gazed up at him, aware that his face seemed familiar to her, yet she was unable to place him. He'd inclined his head in the respectful manner of a well-bred gentleman. Yet when he looked at her, his light blue eyes held a wariness that unsettled her. It was almost as if he were judging her, though for what she couldn't imagine. "I'm sorry, I—"

"Permit me to introduce myself." He gave her a courteous little bow. "My name is Edward Sandringham, at your service."

She recognized the name. From what Baxter had told her, Edward Sandringham was not only new to the Pennyfoot, but until quite recently he had been out of the country. She couldn't have met him before.

"Ah, yes," she murmured. "Mr. Sandringham. I saw your name on the list of reservations. I apologize for not welcoming you earlier. I try to make a habit of personally greeting a first-time guest."

"Please, think nothing of it. I am quite sure you must have more pressing tasks to attend to than my welfare. I can assure you, your maids have taken very good care of my needs so far."

He smiled, and again she had a strong feeling that she had seen this man before somewhere. Yet nowhere in her memory could she place him.

"You have an excellent establishment here, Mrs. Sinclair." Sandringham gazed around him with intense interest on his pleasant face. "How many guest rooms does the hotel have all together?"

Usually only too willing to talk about the hotel's amenities, Cecily was now in a hurry. She did not want to keep Baxter waiting again. Yet courtesy dictated that she at least answer his question. "There are thirty-five, including the six suites."

"Really! More than I'd imagined. The ballroom also serves as the dining room, I understand."

Cecily glanced at the clock. "Yes. We set the tables around the edge of the floor for the dancing. I'm sorry, Mr. Sandringham, but I really must—"

"I expect you keep the rooms well occupied during the

summer, since the hotel is in fairly close proximity to London."

"Usually, yes." Not for much longer, Cecily added inwardly, if trouble insisted on rearing its ugly head at the Pennyfoot.

"What about the winter, though? Do you get many visitors then?"

Now her impatience was edged with uneasiness. He was asking too many direct questions. She had the impression that he was attempting to ferret out something, though she had no idea what that could be. What could he possibly want to know about the hotel that could be of such importance to him?

Whatever it was, he was not about to learn it from her. "I'm afraid you must excuse me, Mr. Sandringham. I have a rather pressing engagement—"

"There you are, Cecily! I was hoping to see you before I left!"

No, not again. Cecily watched Phoebe approach, her face burning with curiosity as she eyed the elegant gentleman at the foot of the stairs. She would have to introduce her friend, of course, Cecily thought gloomily. And she could hardly abandon Phoebe in the next instant. She would have to linger for at least a minute or two. It seemed as if Baxter was once more destined to wait for her.

Gertie stepped out into the yard, burning with resentment that she should be the one sent to find Miss Slowcoach Emily. As if she didn't have enough to do. She was hoping to get through her work fast enough so that she'd at least have a minute or two to talk to Ross before she had to settle the babies down for the night.

She hadn't had a chance to speak to him again since he'd arrived. It was bleeding frustrating to have him so close by and not be able to spend some precious time with him.

She was about to cross the yard to the cellar when she noticed a man standing against the far wall of the hotel, looking around the corner in the direction of the croquet lawns. She couldn't see what he was looking at, but whatever it was held his interest. Until she started to cross the yard, that was.

The heels of her Oxfords rapped out on the stones as she marched sturdily toward the cellar door. She was almost there when out of the corner of her eye she saw the man turn and look at her. Her heart gave a nasty thump when she saw who it was.

Sid Evans grinned at her as he sauntered toward her. "Whoa there, me buxom beauty. Where are you going in such a hurry, then?"

"None of yer bleeding business," Gertie snapped, abandoning all pretense of respect. In her way of thinking, as long as she was outside the hotel walls, she didn't have to be nice to any guest, especially someone as slimy as Sid Evans.

She lost some of her conviction, however, when Sid reached her and took hold of her arm in a bruising grip. "I thought you maids were paid to be nice to the guests," he said in a voice that sent a chill all the way down her back.

"Yeah? Well, you was wrong, weren't you."

"Was I? What if I complained to Mrs. Sinclair that you had been insolent and insulting to me? How long do you think you'd keep your job, then?"

Gertie tugged her arm in a futile attempt to break his grip. "Leggo of me. You're bleeding hurting me."

"I don't have to hurt you. Not if you're nice to me." His hand snaked out and touched her bosom.

Filled with fury, Gertie raised her free hand. "Why, you filthy—"

Sid caught her hand in midair, laughing down at her. "Quite the little spitfire, aren't you, love."

Gertie lifted her chin and spat full into his face.

Sid's laugh disappeared at once. "You shouldn't have done that," he muttered, tightening his grip painfully on her arm. "That wasn't nice at all."

Incensed beyond measure, Gertie opened her mouth and let out a string of curses at the top of her voice. So furious was she, she failed to hear the voice that rang out across the yard. Sid must have heard it, though, as he let her go and turned to face this new threat like an angry lion distracted from his prey.

Following his gaze, Gertie's heart leapt in relief at the sight of Ross striding across the yard toward them. Much as she hated to admit it, the bastard had scared her half to death.

"What's going on here?" Ross demanded, coming to a halt in front of Sid Evans with his bushy brows drawn ferociously together. "Just what do ye think you're doing to this lassie?"

Sid Evans lifted his hands in mock defeat and laughed. "Nothing, guvnor. Just having a bit of fun, that's all. No harm done."

Ross looked at Gertie, who stood rubbing the sore spot on her arm where Sid Evans's fingers had bitten into her. "Did he hurt ye, lass?" he demanded with a look of such concern that Gertie immediately felt better. "If he did, I swear I'll—"

The last thing she wanted was trouble for Ross on his first day. She shook her head, managing to give Sid Evans a baleful glance at the same time. "I'm all right."

" 'Course she's all right." Sid Evans touched his forehead in farewell. "I'll see you later on, Gertie."

"Not if I can bleeding help it," Gertie muttered as she watched him disappear around the corner of the building.

"What was all that about?" Ross asked, his eyes raking Gertie's face as if to assure himself that she was all right. "Was that chap bothering you?"

Gertie shrugged. "I can take care of meself. Been doing it long enough, haven't I."

"I'm not so sure about that." Ross crossed his arms, his expression stern. "Ye know what I think, lass? I think you need someone around to protect you, and that's a fact."

Her heart started banging again, the way it had when she'd

first set eyes on him. It wasn't like her to be bold where
men were concerned. She could tell them off with the best
of them, but when it came to flirting, she wasn't any good
at it.

But when she looked into Ross's kind hazel eyes and saw
the way he looked at her, the words just seemed to trip right
off her tongue. "You wouldn't be offering for the job, would
you?"

Her heart seemed to stop beating again when he moved
closer to her. Even without touching her, he managed to
make her stomach go all quivery. "Aye, that I am, lass,"
he said softly. "In case you have forgotten, I asked you to
be my wife that last time we were together. That offer still
stands. I hafna changed my mind about that."

She didn't know what to say. Her hands felt cold, yet her
face had to be as red as the coals in the kitchen ovens. Her
stomach was all over the place, and her tongue felt as if it
were too big for her mouth.

Ross was still looking at her, waiting for her to say something. She found her voice, though it sounded nothing like
her own when she said weakly, "I'll have to think about it,
all right?"

His grin made her feel a little better. "Aye, ye do that,
lass. And when you've made up your mind, you come and
tell me." He spun on his heel and strode off, and Gertie
could swear she heard the faint echo of bagpipes in the air
as he rounded the corner.

Shaking her head, she made an effort to collect her
thoughts. She was supposed to be doing something. Oh, yes.
She was supposed to see what was keeping that little twit,
Emily. Wouldn't bloody surprise her if she found the maid
lying on the floor sozzled, with an open bottle of wine next
to her. Them quiet ones were the bleeding worst, that's what.

Muttering under her breath, Gertie opened the door to the
cellar and grabbed one of the lamps off the wall. She took
down the box of matches from the ledge and struck one,
setting it to the oil-soaked wick until it caught.

She turned up the wick as high as it would go. She never had liked going down in the cellars. It was worse now, what with some of the horrible types what went down the card rooms lately. She never knew when she was going to meet one of them.

The thought of Flora lying in that bathtub with the life squeezed out of her crossed her mind, and she shuddered. The sooner she found Emily and got out of the creepy cellars, the better.

Gertie reached the foot of the steps and held the lamp above her head. The rows of racks holding the dust-covered wine bottles made it impossible to see where Emily might be, but Gertie caught a glimpse of lamplight at the other end of the cellar.

Trust the blinking twit to be at the wrong end. No wonder she was taking so long. She was looking in the wrong place. The red wine for dinner that night was behind the steps, right under Gertie's nose. In fact, she distinctly remembered Mrs. Chubb telling Emily where to find it.

Gertie took a few steps into the cellar and yelled at the top of her voice. "Emily? Get over here, you silly twit."

She waited, but all she could hear was the faint drip of water somewhere. Cursing under her breath, she moved deeper into the cellar. "Come on, Emily, for Gawd's sake. I've got to get back to the kitchen."

Still she heard no sound. Her skin was beginning to creep now. Her voice had carried the length of the cellar. Emily would have to be deaf not to hear her. Or asleep. She refused to think of the third alternative.

Even so, the minute she saw Emily's bare foot sticking out from behind one of the racks, she had an idea what she would find. Samuel had been very thorough when giving them the gory details about Flora.

Holding her breath, Gertie drew closer, until she was level with the end of the rack. "Emily?" Her quivering voice sounded loud as it bounced off the stone walls. Emily, however, was past hearing it.

The lantern leaned against the wall, as if thrown there by a careless hand. In the glow from the flickering flame, Emily's face looked an odd shade of blue. She lay on her back, completely nude, her clothes in a neat pile beside her. Around her neck, she wore one black stocking, wound so tight the skin bulged beneath it.

Gertie took one look and was violently sick.

"You really must come and visit the church," Phoebe said, fluttering her eyelashes at Edward Sandringham. "It is over four hundred years old and in marvelous condition, all things considered."

"I should like that very much." He glanced at Cecily. "Do you go down to the church very often, Mrs. Sinclair?"

Cecily's insides were beginning to churn at the amount of time that was passing, but she managed to say pleasantly, "As often as the hotel business allows."

"Of course. I don't suppose you get much time to go anywhere. How many staff do you employ in the hotel? It must take a great number to keep a hotel like this running smoothly."

"It certainly does," Cecily said shortly. She was beginning to resent the probing questions and had no intention of answering the man. "I'm sorry, Phoebe, Mr. Sandringham, but I really must attend to my business now. If you will excuse me?"

Phoebe nodded, then looked past Cecily up the stairs. "Mr. Baxter! Just the person I wanted to see. I wonder if I might—"

Whatever she was going to ask never made it past her lips as it became apparent by Baxter's grim expression that he was not in the best of moods. "Well, perhaps another time," Phoebe added lamely. "I really should be going, in any case. Algie will wonder where I am."

She turned to Edward Sandringham, who was watching with great interest as Baxter descended the stairs. "It was such a pleasure to meet you, Mr. Sandringham." She offered her hand in a delicate gesture and was obviously quite thrilled when he took her gloved fingers and pressed them to his lips.

"Likewise, I'm sure," he murmured.

Cecily barely noticed the byplay. She was too concerned with Baxter's expression as he drew near the bottom of the steps. Deciding to take the bull by the horns, she said loudly, "I was on my way to our appointment, Baxter, when Mr. Sandringham waylaid me." She sent what she hoped was a meaningful look at Baxter. "Have you made his acquaintance yet?"

Baxter paused at the foot of the stairs and gave Edward Sandringham a hard look. "Charmed, I'm sure."

The other man held out his hand. "I'm happy to meet you, Baxter. I was just telling Mrs. Sinclair how impressed I am with this hotel. I congratulate you both."

Baxter looked slightly mollified as he took the man's hand and gave it a firm shake.

"I'll be running along now," Phoebe said, sending another shy glance at Edward Sandringham. "I hope to see you at St. Bartholomews on Sunday."

"I'll be there." Sandringham smiled at her, then turned back to Cecily. "Forgive me, but I have some business to attend to myself. At what hour will dinner be served?"

Just as he spoke, the grandfather clock chimed the hour. "In about half an hour," Baxter said, sounding just a trifle stiff. "You will have time for a cocktail in the bar, if you choose."

"Thank you. I do believe I will." Sandringham looked at Cecily and inclined his head. "Mrs. Sinclair, may I say that it has been a very great pleasure indeed to meet you."

In spite of her misgivings about the man, Cecily couldn't help feeling somewhat disarmed. "That is most kind, Mr. Sandringham."

Baxter cleared his throat, making it sound almost like a growl. He was silent as the tall gentleman walked swiftly down the hallway and out of sight.

"Baxter—" Cecily began, but he halted her with a quick shake of his head.

"It is no use, Cecily. We are obviously not going to have any peace and quiet as long as we are in the hotel. I will order a trap for us after the evening meal, and we will go up to the Downs. It is quite pleasant up there in the moonlight. Perhaps there I shall have enough privacy to propose to you in the proper manner."

Feeling sorry for him, as well as herself, Cecily laid her hand on his arm. "Bax, it really isn't necessary, you know. I shan't mind if our betrothal does not follow the traditional procedure. After all, everything else is changing in this modern world, why not that?"

"Because, my dear madam, some things never change. I have waited a very long time for this moment and I will not be robbed of the solemnity of it. I might be forced to change my thinking in some respects, but by God, when I propose to my woman and wait breathlessly for her answer, I want to be alone with her on bended knee."

Secretly thrilled by the passion behind his words, Cecily reminded him gently, "You already have proposed, you know."

Baxter stretched his neck above his collar. "I was interrupted the last time before we could conclude our assignation. You had not given me your answer. I will not allow that to happen again."

She felt ridiculously close to tears. He was so determined to do things properly. Dear Baxter. No matter how the world changed, part of him would always remain steeped in the old ways. She wouldn't have it any other way. "I would love to go with you to Putney Downs, Baxter."

"You will let nothing prevent you this time?"

"I promise."

"Very well, then. Perhaps we can dine together first. I should be finished with my duties in about half an hour. I'll order a bottle of our favorite wine."

"I'd like that." Thinking of the wine reminded her of

Emily. "I think I'll run back to the kitchen for a moment," she said as Baxter turned to go. "I'll meet you in the dining room."

He didn't exactly smile, but his expression was much less severe when he left.

Cecily made her way to the kitchen, her anticipation of her imminent engagement uppermost in her mind. She was smiling when she pushed the kitchen door open. The smile soon vanished, however, when she saw Gertie standing by the door to the yard, her face as white as bleached linen and streaked with tears.

Mrs. Chubb turned to look at Cecily as she entered, and she knew at once by the housekeeper's expression that something dreadful had happened. She wasn't totally surprised when Gertie burst into sobs, almost drowning out the housekeeper's hushed words.

"It's Emily, mum. She's been strangled with her own stocking. Just like bleeding Flora."

CHAPTER

9

"Thank heavens we decided to close the gaming rooms to-night," Baxter said when Cecily went to his office to deliver the bad news. "Though how we can expect to keep two murders a secret from our guests I cannot imagine."

"I expect the inspector will want to question everybody in the hotel when he arrives in the morning," Cecily said gloomily. "Including the guests."

"No doubt." Baxter looked up from the ledger he was examining and gave her a sharp look. "I trust you are not thinking about beating him to the punch?"

She tried not to look too guilty. "As a matter of fact, I did think I'd have a word with Gertie. You know how she hates talking to the inspector. She simply forgets everything she saw or heard. Perhaps if I talk to her tonight, she can shed some light on this. Two murders in the same day, Baxter. It has to be someone in this hotel. I just can't imagine why someone would want to kill two of my maids—''

She stopped short, remembering her conversation with Pansy earlier. "The prophet! For heaven's sake, how could I have forgotten. That could be why Emily was killed."

Baxter looked alarmed. "What are you talking about?"

"I was going to mention this to you, in any case, but what with everything happening, it went clean out of my head."

Baxter replaced the pen in the inkstand and leaned back. "Well, perhaps you'd better tell me about it now."

"Pansy told me she'd seen a strange man wandering around the Pennyfoot. He wore a beard and had strange eyes, according to her. He kept insisting that the world was coming to an end and that she had to prepare herself."

"As far as I am aware, there is no guest in the hotel wearing a beard." Baxter leaned forward and stroked his eyelids with his fingers. "I knew we should have replaced Ned right away. The doors of the Pennyfoot are open to any vagrant who cares to wander in at will. Still, that doesn't necessarily mean that he's the murderer. Usually those kind of people go to the kitchen and ask for food, and then go on their way."

"Well, yes, that's what I thought, too. I thought that it was just a matter of the girls overreacting. But Pansy didn't see this man in the kitchen. She saw him wandering around in the hallways. And so did Emily. I wonder now if Emily saw something she wasn't supposed to see. Perhaps she saw this man near the bathroom where Flora was killed, and he strangled her, too, so that she couldn't incriminate him."

Baxter narrowed his eyes. "If that's the case, Cecily, I absolutely forbid you to go searching for a possible murderer. P.C. Northcott will be here later this evening, and he can conduct a search of the hotel."

"By then the killer might have escaped, or worse, murdered yet another of my maids. We must look for this suspect as soon as possible. Now. I'll get Samuel on it right away."

"Cecily!" Baxter's voice was sharp as he rose from his chair. "Inspector Cranshaw has taken a very dim view of your interference as he calls it. His last warning stated quite plainly that if you continued to meddle in police affairs, he would not only close down the hotel, he would also put you in jail for a while to teach you a lesson.''

''Piffle.'' Cecily tossed her head. ''There isn't one judge in the country who would put a lady in prison for fulfilling her obligation to those in her trust.''

For answer, Baxter picked up the daily newspaper lying on his desk and showed her the front page. The headlines proclaimed in large black letters that a suffragette had died of starvation while conducting a hunger strike in prison. ''These days the judges are only too happy to imprison women for their disruption of the peace. I would suggest, Cecily, that you consider long and hard before embarking on another of your dangerous investigations.''

She stared at him in frustration. ''Baxter, do you not understand the situation here? The Pennyfoot is in deep trouble, both financially and morally. We are forced to close down our biggest avenue of income, the card rooms. Our customary guests, the members of the aristocracy who have been our mainstay for many years, are deserting us for more exotic climates, and it is nigh impossible to find decent domestic help nowadays.

''Now we have a double murder on our hands, committed on the same day by the same hand, no doubt, and more than likely a person on these premises. If I can do anything to speed the apprehension of whoever did this, possibly saving the lives of my staff and undoubtedly securing the reputation of this hotel, then I must follow whatever course is open to me. And to blazes with Inspector Cranshaw.''

''Endangering yourself in the process. Have you no regard for your own safety? Have you no thought as to my feelings if something should happen to you?''

''Nothing is going to happen to me, Baxter. I am not stupid. I am and always have been cautious in my conduct.''

''If I remember, the very last time you took it upon yourself to investigate a murder, you were almost suffocated in a dentist chair.''

''That was an exception.''

''Indeed. And what will happen if I am not close by should there be another exception?''

Cecily let out her breath in an explosive sigh. ''Baxter, you worry entirely too much. I give you my solemn promise I shall not embark upon any course of action that might endanger my life. All I want to do now is to ask a few questions and organize a search for this man, on the chance he could be involved in the murder. I will send whatever staff we can spare on the search and make sure they are not alone.''

He gave her one of his frosty glares, but she held her ground. She was not about to let him forbid her to do anything. No matter if he was acting in regard for her safety. This was something that would have to be understood between them. Although this was obviously not the time to discuss it, she thought, looking at his icy expression.

For a long, tense moment they glared at each other, then Baxter said coldly, ''I assume our trip to the Downs will have to be cancelled?''

His words were such an anticlimax she felt like laughing, and might well have done so had the situation not been so serious.

''I'm sorry, Baxter,'' she said evenly. ''I realize this is a great disappointment to you, as it is to me. I am quite sure, however, that you will agree with me when I say that this is not a good time to plan such a joyous occasion. Perhaps it would be prudent if we postpone our plans until after this problem is resolved.''

His face grew darker, and the look in his eyes gave her deep cause for concern. ''As you will. I must simply accustom myself to the fact that the Pennyfoot will always take precedence over my needs and my wishes. Perhaps, under the circumstances, we should postpone our plans indefinitely.''

She disguised her pain behind a flash of anger. "Now you are being childish."

"And you, madam, are being stubborn."

She stared at him in painful frustration for a moment or two, then said quietly, "I can see there is no point in discussing this further. I will see that you are informed if any news should arise. Dr. Prestwick will be here shortly to examine poor Emily's body, and I might learn something from him."

"Naturally," Baxter said dryly.

Exasperated, she made a growling sound in her throat and turned to leave.

He spoke her name as she reached the door.

She paused, one hand on the door handle, reluctant to turn and face him again in fear that he would see her tears.

"I do not wish for you to leave me like this, Cecily. I apologize for losing my temper. It is only my intense fear for your safety that prompts me to speak to you in such a manner."

She nodded, longing to run to him, and knowing she must not. "Thank you, Baxter. I do appreciate your concern. I am truly sorry for upsetting you this way. Please believe me when I say I find no joy in it."

She opened the door and slipped through, closing it gently behind her. Feeling only a trifle better, she made her way quickly down the hallway, intent on organizing a search as soon as possible.

Gertie glanced up at the clock on the mantelpiece and cursed under her breath. More than ever now she wanted a word with Ross. Just seeing his comforting presence would help get her nerves back together again, she was just sure of it.

All that upset over finding poor Emily had put her behind with her work. To make matters worse, her hands wouldn't stop shaking, and she kept dropping things.

Everyone was in a terrible mood. Pansy acted as if she expected to be struck down any second, Mrs. Chubb acted as if the whole bleeding thing was her fault, and Michel acted as if he was the only one doing any work.

Gertie picked up the tray of wine glasses, wincing when they rattled and tinkled as she carried them across the kitchen.

"Where are you going with those?" Mrs. Chubb demanded before she'd reached the door.

Gertie threw a glance over her shoulder. "The dining room. They was supposed to be on the tables for dinner but they never got there." She swallowed past a huge lump in her throat when she thought about the reason the glasses weren't on the table.

As if reading her thoughts, Mrs. Chubb asked angrily, "Why weren't they there for dinner? Do I have to think of everything around here? Why can't you girls think for yourselves once in a blue moon?"

Gertie turned so sharply the glasses toppled, sending several of them crashing to the floor. Heedless of the splintered glass at her feet, Gertie yelled, "Because the girl what was supposed to take them in there is lying on the cellar floor with a stocking around her blinking neck, that's why!"

Mrs. Chubb's face turned white. She held out her hands and in a broken voice said, "Oh, I'm sorry, luv. I don't know what's the matter with me, honest I don't."

It was too much for Gertie. She could take Michel's banging, she could take Pansy's whining, she could take the housekeeper's yelling, but Mrs. Chubb being kind to her just finished her. She let go of the tray, and the rest of the glasses shattered on the floor as she opened her mouth and howled.

Mrs. Chubb jumped into action immediately. Yelling at Gertie not to move, she rushed for a dustpan and brush and swept up all the broken glass while Gertie stood and bawled like a baby.

"There, there," the housekeeper kept murmuring while she worked. "Let it all out. It'll do you good, it will."

Gertie didn't know how much good it was going to do her, but she didn't seem able to stop the torrent of tears.

Finally the floor was swept clean, Pansy had been sent to clear the dining room tables, Michel had retreated to the pantry—no doubt to knock back what was left of the cognac—and Gertie was seated on a kitchen chair, blowing her nose into her apron.

For once Mrs. Chubb didn't tell her off. "I know it was a nasty shock for you, duck," she said, putting a hot cup of tea on the table in front of her. "Here, drink this. I slipped some of Michel's rum into it."

Gertie sniffed at the tea. She didn't normally drink booze, but right now her insides were shaking so bad she'd do anything to stop it. "Sorry about the glasses," she muttered.

"Don't you worry about it, duck. We'll work something out, though some of it will have to come out of your wages, I'm afraid."

Gertie sniffed. "Well, I'll be able to bleeding afford it if I don't have to pay Daisy for looking after the babies."

"Well, Daisy hasn't gone yet, has she. There's still time for her to change her mind. She'll find it hard to leave those two beautiful babies, you mark my words."

"I don't know." Gertie's mouth sagged as she looked up at the housekeeper. "It's just like nothing is going flipping right anymore."

Mrs. Chubb gave her a determined smile. "Well, one thing is going right. Your Ross has come back, hasn't he? That's something going right, isn't it?"

"Yeah, I s'pose so." Gertie sniffed again.

Mrs. Chubb peered at her with an anxious frown. "Here, he hasn't said anything to hurt you, has he?"

"Nah." Gertie lifted the steaming cup and sipped at it experimentally. It didn't taste half bad. She took another sip before setting the cup down on its saucer. "It's just that he's asked me to marry him again, hasn't he."

She hadn't meant to say anything. Somehow the words had just slipped out. Mrs. Chubb clasped her hands against her bosom. "Go on, Gertie! Well, I never. What did you tell him, then?"

"I told him I'd think about it, didn't I."

"Well, have you?"

Gertie shrugged. "I haven't had time yet, have I."

"I don't know what we'll do if you leave the Pennyfoot, too."

"I know," Gertie said miserably. "That's the bloody problem, ain't it."

After a short pause, Mrs. Chubb reached for a chair and pulled it up to the table. Plonking herself down on it, she leaned her elbows on the table and stared into Gertie's face. "Now you listen to me, my girl. This is your whole life we're talking about here. Don't you let nothing stop you from doing what is in your heart to do. The Pennyfoot will get along just fine without you if that's what you want to do."

Gertie felt her bottom lip trembling again and caught it between her teeth. "But what am I going to do without you?" she whispered. "And Madam and Mr. Baxter? You're all my family. My kids' godparents and fill-in grandma."

"You won't have to do without us, will you. Now that Ross is working at the Pennyfoot—"

Gertie shook her head. "He'll go back to Scotland if I marry him. That's what he wants. It's what he's always wanted."

"Well, you'll have your husband and your children, Gertie. And a house to take care of. You won't have no time to miss us, I promise you that."

Gertie felt a sharp pain when she saw a tear form in Mrs. Chubb's eye. She felt even worse when the housekeeper said softly, "I'm going to miss you, too, Gertie. And especially those two little babies, that I am."

Deciding that she'd dealt with enough emotion for one day, Gertie cleared her throat and got to her feet. "Well, I don't have to make up me mind tonight, do I. It's not like he's leaving on the midnight train."

"Don't keep him waiting too long, Gertie." Mrs. Chubb rose and dusted down her apron with her hands. "Ross

McBride is a good man. There's many a woman out there who would be only too happy to take him for a husband.''

"I know." Gertie smiled. "Don't worry, Mrs. Chubb. I'll make up me mind, one way or another, soon."

The housekeeper nodded and turned away. "Speaking of Ross McBride," she said gruffly, "didn't you say you wanted a word with him before settling down with those babies?"

Gertie sighed. "Yeah, I did. But I haven't finished folding the serviettes yet."

"Go along with you. I'll finish them. There aren't that many."

Gertie felt like putting her arms around the plump woman and giving her a big hug. She knew if she did she'd start bawling again, so she said instead, "Thanks, Mrs. Chubb. That's really nice of you. I'll make up for it tomorrow."

"Get out of here before I change my mind."

Gertie wasn't going to wait around for that to happen. She pulled off her apron, dropped it in the laundry basket, and rushed out to find Ross.

She found him in the garden shed, examining the tools crammed in there. The sun had disappeared behind the tall slopes of Putney Downs, but it was still light enough to see inside the shed without a lamp.

"Hello there, lass," he said in his deep voice when she poked her head inside. "I was hoping I'd see you again tonight."

"I can't stop long," Gertie said, slipping inside the shed. "Daisy will be wondering where I am. I'm supposed to settle the babies down for the night in a few minutes."

"I'll be happy to take whatever time you can spare." Ross seized two metal buckets from among the rakes and shovels and turned them both upside down. "Sit down for a minute and tell me what happened in the cellar tonight. Are you all right, lass? Samuel told me you had a nasty shock. Another maid has been murdered, he said?"

Gertie shivered and lowered herself onto the bucket.

"Yeah, it were me what found her. I'll never forget it. She looked so helpless lying there. I've never been so scared in my entire life. I was so scared I couldn't run up the steps fast enough. Bruised both me knees, I did, trying to get out of there."

"Ah, lass, I should have gone down there with you." Ross shifted his bucket closer, sat down, and folded his arms around her.

It wasn't like the last time he did that. That time she'd felt nervous and shaky, all quivery inside. Now all she felt was a deep sense of peace, as if she'd come home after a long, long journey.

Shaken by the feeling, she pulled away from him. "There was no need for you to come down with me," she said offhandedly. "I done it all the time on me own. How was anyone to know that there'd be Emily's dead body down there?"

As if sensing her confusion, Ross shifted away from her. "I still say you need protecting. Every woman does, no matter how strong she is."

Gertie thought about that. "Well, I'm not going to say as how it isn't a nice idea. It does make me feel better knowing someone cares about what happens to me."

"So why don't you marry me, lass? You know I'll take right good care of you and the wee bairns, that I will. I'll make sure that nothing bad ever happens to you again. Not if I can help it, anyway."

She stared at him, wondering why she couldn't just say yes and be done with it. She didn't know what was holding her back, but something was. Maybe it was her bad experience with Ian, finding out he was married to someone else when all the time she'd thought she was his proper wife.

Or maybe it was because she was afraid to leave the only home she knew and take her babies so far away with a man she didn't know at all. All she knew was that she wasn't sure, and until she was, she wasn't going to marry no one.

"I can't," she said, feeling more miserable than she ever remembered.

"Are ye telling me you can't marry me?"

Tears filled her eyes at the sadness in his voice. She shook her head. "All I'm saying right now is that I don't know what to do."

He nodded, his face serious. "All right, I'll give you some time. But I have to tell ye, lass, if you turn me down again, I'll be going back to Scotland. It wouldna be fair to either of us to go on like this. If I go back without you, Gertie, I promise you you'll never hear from me again."

She knew he meant it. She also knew what it would do to her if he went out of her life. Yet try as she would, she couldn't say the words that would tie her to him forever. And that was the saddest thing that had happened to her that day.

CHAPTER
❀ 10 ❀

It had been a long day, Cecily thought as she walked once more down the steps to the kitchen. Dr. Prestwick had been able to tell her nothing more about the second murder, except that one of Emily's shoes was missing. Just like Flora's.

As for P.C. Northcott, he had gone down to the cellar muttering about how upset Inspector Cranshaw was going to be when he found out he had two murders on his hands.

Cecily didn't need reminding of that fact. Things were beginning to look extremely bleak indeed for the Pennyfoot. What she needed was a nice cup of tea to soothe her frayed nerves.

Mrs. Chubb looked up from the stove when she walked in. "I was just heating up some milk, mum. Would you care for some? With a spoonful of brandy, perhaps?"

Cecily sank onto the hard seat of a kitchen chair. "You

know, Altheda, I think I will. It might help me to sleep tonight.''

''I reckon we all need something to help us sleep this night,'' Mrs. Chubb muttered as she poured the steaming milk into two mugs. ''This has been a terrible day. Two young girls barely more than babies, snuffed out before they had a chance to know what life was all about. Wicked it is.''

Her last words sounded strained as she reached up to a cupboard and took down a bottle half full of brandy.

Cecily waited while the housekeeper poured a spoonful of the golden liquor into each mug, stirred them both, and carried them to the table. ''Here, mum,'' she said, putting one down in front of Cecily, ''this will chase away the colly-wobbles in your stomach.''

''Thank you, Altheda.'' Cecily cautiously took a sip of the hot brew. ''Has Gertie gone to her room for the night?''

''Not yet, mum.'' Mrs. Chubb gave her a wan smile. ''She's gone to have a word with that nice Mr. McBride.''

Cecily eyed the housekeeper with apprehension. ''Do you think there's a possibility of an attachment between them?''

''It's hard to say, mum.''

''But it is possible?''

The housekeeper sighed. ''I might as well tell you, mum. Mr. McBride has asked Gertie to marry him. Gertie doesn't know what she wants to do about it yet, so I'd really be grateful if you wouldn't mention it to her just yet.''

Cecily nodded, trying in vain to feel happy for Gertie. ''Of course, Altheda. Though once she makes up her mind, I'd like to know at once, so that we can attempt to replace her.'' She picked up her mug and took a strong gulp of the stuff. ''Though how in the world we are going to replace Gertie I haven't the faintest idea.''

''I know, mum. It's a bit of a worry, isn't it. What with Daisy going, as well—''

''Daisy?'' Cecily stared at the housekeeper in dismay. ''Daisy is leaving?''

''Yes, mum. I'm sorry, I forgot she hadn't told you yet.

She wants to go to London to be with her sister.''

Cecily shook her head. "I should have expected it. What will Gertie do without her to look after the babies?"

"I don't know, mum," Mrs. Chubb said, sounding worried. "I only hope she doesn't agree to marry Mr. McBride for the wrong reasons. I—"

She broke off as the door to the yard burst open and Gertie erupted into the kitchen. The housemaid halted at the sight of Cecily and dropped a clumsy curtsey. "Sorry, mum. I didn't know you was here."

She sounded breathless, and Cecily peered at her across the room. "Are you all right, Gertie?"

"Yes, mum. At least, I would be if I hadn't found that poor Emily dead on the cellar floor."

"Of course. I'm sorry, Gertie. That must have been a nasty shock for you."

Gertie looked as if she were about to cry. "It were that, mum. Me and Daisy both. I can't believe them two little girls is gone. They was both so chipper yesterday, they was. It just goes to show how easy it bleeding happens. Here one day, gone the next."

"Well, I'm sure Madam doesn't want to talk about it anymore," Mrs. Chubb said, rising to her feet. "It's time you were taking care of those babies, Gertie."

"Actually I would like to ask you one or two questions, Gertie, before you go." Cecily patted the empty chair next to her. "Come and sit down. You look all in."

"I am, mum. Thank you ever so much." Gertie sat on the edge of her chair as if she were committing a mortal sin.

"I want to know if you've seen this strange man who frightened Emily so much," Cecily said after she'd drained the rest of her brandy-laced milk. "I understand he was seen by both Emily and Pansy."

"Yes, mum. I mean no, mum. I haven't seen him." Gertie frowned. "Pansy said as how he kept telling them the world was coming to an end. I reckon it bloody well did for Flora and Emily. You think he's the one what done it?"

"I don't know, Gertie. I've asked Samuel to organize a search for the man, though I really don't expect we shall find him at this late hour. He most likely has left the Pennyfoot by now."

"He's not one of the guests?" Mrs. Chubb asked, looking alarmed. "I didn't take that much notice of Pansy when she mentioned him. I thought it was someone having a bit of fun. You know how some guests like to tease the maids."

"Well, all I can say right now is that I'll feel a lot better when we've found him and questioned him." Cecily hid a yawn behind her hand. "Oh, excuse me. Gertie, did you see anything strange when you went down to the cellar to fetch Emily?"

Gertie shook her head. "No, mum. Not that I was taking a lot of notice. I was still fuming over what that Sid Evans did. I swear, if Ross hadn't been there I'd have bleeding—"

"Gertie!" Mrs. Chubb warned. "Watch your mouth."

Cecily shook her head at the housekeeper. "It's all right, Mrs. Chubb." She turned once more to Gertie. "What is this about Sid Evans?"

Gertie's face flushed. "Well, I met him in the yard. He was rude to me, touched me where he shouldn't, he did, and Ross came over and told him off." A smile softened Gertie's strong features. "He was so masterful. Sent that 'orrible Sid Evans off with a bl—flea in his ear, he did."

Cecily frowned. "Whatever was Mr. Evans doing in the kitchen yard?"

"I don't know, mum." Gertie looked thoughtful. "Come to think of it, he did look a bit strange. He was peering around the corner of the building, like he was watching someone." Her eyes widened. "Maybe he saw the bloke what done Emily in!"

"Well, I shall have to ask him about that." Cecily yawned again and looked up at the clock. "But not tonight. I imagine by now everyone will be asleep." She got to her feet, aware of the deep weariness creeping over her. "I'm going to my suite, Mrs. Chubb. Samuel should be finished with the search very shortly. I told him to report to Baxter if he discovered the man, but I really don't think he will find him tonight.''

''Very well, mum.''

''If anything should happen—''

''I'll see that word gets to you right away, mum.''

Cecily gave her a tired smile. ''Thank you, Altheda.'' She left the kitchen, nursing the fervent hope that she would not be disturbed until morning.

Daisy was up bright and early the next morning. She had written to Doris the night before and told her about her decision to move to London. Now that she'd really made up her mind, she couldn't wait to get things started and had asked Doris to watch out for a nanny's job for her. Maybe Bella DelRay knew of someone who needed a nanny.

Daisy dressed in a hurry and slipped the letter into her apron pocket. She just had time to run down the esplanade to the postbox and get back before Gertie had to start work in the kitchen.

Creeping down the quiet hallway, she held her breath when a floorboard creaked right outside Mrs. Chubb's room. The housekeeper didn't take kindly to being disturbed before the proper time, and Daisy had no wish to explain why she was in such a hurry to post a letter.

She wanted to catch the morning collection. The sooner the letter was on its way, the sooner she could start her new life in London. Daisy felt like skipping with excitement as she reached the top of the stairs and crossed the foyer.

The heavy oak door was always locked at night. Usually Samuel was the first one to unlock it, on his way to tend to the horses. This morning, however, Daisy had beaten him to it.

She lifted the heavy latch and eased it into its slot. Slowly she eased the thick bolts back, making sure they were clear of the door. The big iron key hung on a hook on the wall, and she took it down and fitted it into the keyhole. It turned easily, and she breathed a sigh of relief.

Her sigh changed to a gasp, however, when the door swung open to reveal a man huddled on the doorstep. He straightened when he heard her and turned to face her.

His features were partially hidden by a thick bushy beard, and his eyes glowed like black coals as he stared at her. He wasn't a big man, but there was something menacing about the way he stood very still, watching her.

"What do you want?" Daisy asked sharply before she remembered her manners. "I mean, to whom did you wish to speak?" She kept her hand on the door, just in case she had to slam it in his face. After all, it was much too early for any visitors to be arriving. In any case, he didn't look like a visitor. He didn't have any luggage with him, for one thing.

He didn't answer her, but just stood there, with that weird expression in his eyes. There was no way she was going to go out there and try to pass him. Instead, she made her voice sound like Mrs. Chubb's. "If you don't wish to speak to anyone, then please get off these steps. Or I shall be forced to call the manager."

He moved then and took a step toward her.

Daisy moved back and half closed the door. Peering at him through the gap, she said loudly, "There's no one here at the moment. You'll have to come back later if you want to speak to someone."

The man lifted his hand and pointed at her. In a hollow voice, he chanted, "You must prepare yourself to meet your Maker."

For a minute she didn't know what he meant. Then, as his meaning sank in, she went cold with fright. The vision of Flora lying naked in the bathtub was clear in her mind. She knew she should close the door, but somehow her hand wouldn't move. She could only stand and gawk at the man, frozen in terror.

His trembling hand still pointed at her, and his eyes grew

wide and fierce. "The end is near!" he cried out. "You must prepare. The world is coming to an end." He took another step toward her, releasing her numbed mind. With a little yelp of fright, she slammed the door and slid the bolts across with a satisfying and quite deafening crash of metal.

"Strewth, Daisy, do you have to make such a blinking racket?"

Samuel's voice behind her gave her an even worse fright, and she shrieked as she spun around to face him. "Gawd, Samuel, you scared me half to death." She patted her heart, which was galloping like a runaway horse.

Samuel shook his head. "What are you doing up so early, anyway?"

"Sshh!" She put her finger to her lips. "There's a man outside, and I think he's the one what killed Flora."

Samuel's eyes widened. "How'd you know? Who is he?"

Daisy pointed frantically at the door. "He's out there now. He told me I had to prepare to meet my Maker. He said the world was coming to an end."

She jumped in fright again as Samuel leapt past her and slid back the bolts. He swung the door open, and she scrambled back to the top of the kitchen steps. "Don't let him in!" she yelled. "He'll kill us!"

Paying no heed to her warning, Samuel plunged through the door and out of sight.

Daisy stood trembling at the top of the steps, one hand pressed against her mouth to stop her scream from escaping. She desperately wanted to know what was happening out there, but was too terrified to take a look.

She could hear nothing beyond the door. No shouts, no sounds of a scuffle. Still she stood, waiting in the fearful silence for Samuel to return.

At last he stepped back inside the foyer, his chest heaving with exertion. "I couldn't see him anywhere," he said, struggling to catch his breath between the words. "Did you get a good look at him?"

"As plain as the nose on my face." Daisy's knees felt

like they were made of rubber. ''He was standing right in front of me, and he pointed at me like this.'' She extended her finger and pointed at Samuel.

''What did he look like?''

She described him as best as she could remember, and Samuel nodded. ''That's the bloke what I was supposed to find last night. He must have left the hotel before the door was locked, and now he's waiting to come back.''

''Oh, my,'' Daisy moaned. ''He's going to kill us all before he's done.''

''Well, he's certainly not bothering to hide himself, is he.'' Samuel frowned. ''I wonder where he went. I looked down both ends of the esplanade. He couldn't have gone far.''

''More than likely he's still on the grounds,'' Daisy said, feeling sick. ''He's just waiting for another chance to knock another one of us off. We shall have to tell Mr. Baxter right away.''

''I'll do it.'' Samuel looked at her curiously. ''Where was you going, anyway, this early in the morning?''

Daisy pressed her lips together. ''I was going to post a letter,'' she said a little defiantly. ''I wrote to Doris last night.''

''Yeah? What did you tell her?''

''Just that I'd decided I was going to move to London.''

Samuel looked over his shoulder as if he were making sure no one was about to hear him. ''Can you keep a secret?'' he whispered.

She frowned. ''What sort of secret?''

''Promise you won't say nothing to nobody.''

''It won't get me into trouble, will it?''

''Nah, nothing like that. God's honor.''

''All right, I promise. What is it?''

Samuel sent that furtive look around again. ''I'm moving to the Smoke, too.''

Daisy stared at him. ''Go on! When?''

''Soon. I've been writing to Doris, too.''

Daisy eyed him with suspicion. "She never told me."

"Because I told her not to, silly. I made her promise to keep it a secret, too."

"Have you got a job there, then?"

"Not yet." Samuel shrugged. "There's plenty of work for someone what knows how to handle horses, though. I've had offers before from some of the toffs who stayed here. I reckon I could take one of them up on it."

"What does Doris say about it, then?"

"She's happy about it. She told me she gets real lonely in the big city, and she's looking forward to having me around for company."

Daisy nodded. "That's what she told me. Have you told Madam yet?"

Samuel shook his head. "I can't, can I. Not with all this trouble going on. Her and Baxter have enough to worry about without me adding to it. I'll tell them when all this mess is over."

Daisy shuddered. "Well, it won't be over unless you tell Mr. Baxter about that man outside."

Samuel started. "Strewth! I almost forgot all about him, didn't I. I'll go right now and wake him up. Though what he can do about it now the bugger's gone, I don't know."

"He can send for the constable again, that's what."

"The P.C.'s coming back anyway. I heard Madam say last night that the inspector was coming to do an investigation this morning."

"Well, I hope he hurries up," Daisy muttered darkly, "before there's more murders and we're all found dead in our beds."

Samuel laughed as he hurried off, but his laugh sounded weird, echoing down the long hallway as if mocking the two girls who had died so violently at the hands of the unknown killer.

CHAPTER

❈ 11 ❈

Cecily felt quite heavy-hearted as she descended the stairs. It seemed as if her entire world were beginning to topple around her. The deaths of those two young girls had weighed heavily on her mind, preventing her from enjoying a restful night.

The fear of what might lay ahead before this fiend was caught had given her nightmares, and on top of all her worries, she and Baxter were at odds. Although there had been times in the past when they'd had their differences, it was particularly distressing now, when they were on the point of betrothal and should be sharing joy in each other's company.

She reached the foyer and caught sight of Samuel about to depart through the front door. She called out to him, and he turned to hurry back to her.

"Have you had a chance to examine the chimney in Room Seventeen yet?" she asked when he reached her. "If there is something wrong up there, we might as well take care of it as long as the room is empty.''

"No, I haven't mum. I'll do it this morning. Though if you ask me, that Sid Evans is hearing things, more than likely.''

"Well, I'd like to be sure.'' Cecily frowned, remembering Gertie's words last night. "You haven't seen him about this morning, I suppose?''

"Mr. Evans? No, mum, I haven't.'' He hesitated, as if unsure about something, then blurted out, "Daisy saw the bloke we was looking for, though. He was on the doorstep this morning. Scared her half to death, he did.''

Cecily caught her breath. "Where is he now?''

Samuel shrugged. "Don't know, mum. I went after him, like you said, but by the time I got down the steps, he'd vanished.''

"He wasn't on the esplanade?''

"Not as far as I could see.''

"That means he could still be on the grounds some-where.''

Samuel looked apprehensive. "Yes, mum. That's what Mr. Baxter thinks. He sent me to fetch Ross McBride so's we can go look for him.''

Cecily glanced at the clock. "Then hurry, Samuel. The inspector should be here shortly, and I would feel a great deal easier if that man was brought in for questioning.''

"Yes, mum. Right away.'' Samuel touched his forehead with his fingers, then hurried out of the door, closing it behind him with a decisive thud.

Cecily felt almost tempted to lock the door again. That wasn't possible, of course, since it must remain open for the guests to come and go. Nevertheless, she felt very uneasy as she hurried down the hallway to Baxter's office.

She met him coming out of the door, and to her great relief he appeared happy to see her. "I was just on my way to help the men hunt for this prophet fellow whom everyone is talking about," he told her after they'd exchanged greetings.

She couldn't resist a sly comment. "You are not concerned about incurring the inspector's wrath?"

He raised his eyebrows at her. "I am forced to admit, Cecily, that sometimes my caution overrides my common sense."

"Indeed. It isn't often you admit that you are at fault."

"Granted. In this case, however, I might have made too hasty a judgement last night. Samuel's account of Daisy's encounter this morning changed my mind."

"Then you do agree there is cause for concern."

Baxter rocked back on his heels, wearing a pompous expression. "Since several people have met this intruder, and since it appears that he apparently has no business in our hotel other than to frighten people, I think the inspector would agree that the man is a viable suspect in the murders and therefore should be detained in order that his innocence or guilt be established."

"Now you sound like P.C. Northcott."

Baxter groaned. "Please, dear madam, I have quite enough to contend with."

She relented at once. "You're right, Baxter. This is no time for sparring. I just hope you find this man before the inspector arrives. I would hate to have to explain to him that a possible murderer is lurking around the hotel apparently at will."

"I'll keep you informed," Baxter promised. "Please promise me that you will use extreme caution when moving about the hotel."

"Of course." She looked up at him. "It would certainly help matters if this prophet turned out to be the murderer. Then we might still be able to keep the disturbing news from the guests."

"I think that is a forlorn hope, I'm afraid. Once Cranshaw and Northcott get here, there is bound to be speculation. Sooner or later one of the staff is almost certain to let something slip. In any case, the inspector will undoubtedly want to question the guests."

"I suppose so." Her desolation returned, even more oppressive than before. "Oh, Baxter, what are we going to do?"

He reached out a hand, then, apparently aware that they were in a public place, thought better of it. Dropping his hand again, he murmured, "We'll do what we've always done, Cecily. We'll deal with the situation to the best of our ability and trust in divine Providence."

She lifted her chin at his words. "Of course. It has always worked before, hasn't it. Thank you, Baxter."

"Not at all, dear madam." After giving her a long, hard look, he set off down the hallway in his long stride.

She was about to follow more slowly, then decided instead to change direction and head for the dining room. She could think better on a full stomach, and it seemed likely that she would need her wits about her if she was to deal with Inspector Cranshaw.

The minute she entered the dining room she could feel the tension in the air. Pansy fluttered from table to table wearing a set expression and fear in her eyes. Gertie stomped around as if she had the entire world resting on her shoulders, though she managed a tight smile as she approached Cecily's table and dropped a slight curtsey.

The breakfast that morning was a hearty one, starting with porridge, followed by scrambled eggs, sausage, bacon, ham, fried tomatoes, braised kidneys, and thick slices of Mrs. Chubb's baked bread. Cecily managed to eat very little of it, however, and wished Baxter had joined her to share in the meal.

She poured herself a cup of tea from the silver pot and glanced around the dining room. It was too early for most of the guests to be at breakfast, but she caught sight of Sid Evans seated at a corner table, apparently absorbed in the newspaper he had spread out in front of him.

Deciding to take this opportunity to speak with him, Ce-

cily rose from her chair and crossed the room to his table.
"Good morning, Mr. Evans," she said brightly. "I trust you
had a better night last night? No strange noises in your fireplace?"

Sid Evans jumped violently, rattling the newspaper in his
hands. "Ah, Mrs. Sinclair." He got clumsily to his feet.
"Won't you join me?"

"Thank you, Mr. Evans. Most gracious of you." She
waited while he pulled out a chair for her, then sat down
gingerly as he pushed it in behind her.

"I did sleep better, thank you," he said when he'd seated
himself again. "That room at the end of the corridor is most
quiet and peaceful."

"Yes, well there aren't many guests on that floor. Just
you and Brigadier Chatsworth, and the Medlingtons at the
other end."

"Right." His hand strayed to his tie, and he fiddled with
the knot. "Did you ever find out what was making that noise
in the fireplace?"

"Not as yet. Samuel is going up on the roof this morning,
though, for a closer inspection. More than likely it was a
stray owl or some such creature. We don't want anything
stuck in the chimney, however, or we shall have a fine mess
on our hands when we light the fires in the winter."

"I should think so." His gaze flicked over to the door
then back at her face. Leaning forward, he said in a harsh
whisper, "Have they found out who did those poor girls in
yet?"

Cecily started. "How did you hear about that?"

Sid Evans shrugged. "It's all over the hotel. Someone saw
the constable go down the cellar last night and asked one of
the maids. She told him that two of the maids had been
murdered. Caused quite a sensation, she did."

It must have been Pansy, Cecily thought with a flash of
irritation. None of her established staff would have been so
indiscreet. She would have to have a word with the girl and
remind her of the hotel policy—silence at all costs.

Now that he had presented her with the opportunity, however, there didn't seem any point in beating about the bush.
"I understand you spoke to Gertie shortly before she discovered Emily's body," she said, keeping her voice low.

Sid Evans gave her a wary look. "I saw her in the kitchen
yard, if that's what you mean."

Cecily nodded. "I was just wondering how you came to
be in the yard yesterday evening. Our guests don't usually
wander around in the domestic quarters. Unless they are
looking for something, of course. Or perhaps . . . someone?"

"Actually I was trying to avoid someone."

This wasn't quite what she'd expected. "Oh, really? Not
one of my staff, I hope?"

"One of your guests, as a matter of fact." Sid Evans
reached a languid hand across the table. "Care for some
tea?"

"Not at present, thank you."

She watched him pour the tea. A few drops splashed into
the saucer and onto the white linen tablecloth. He dabbed at
the stain with his serviette, his face expressionless.

"Mr. Evans," Cecily said carefully, "if you are having
problems with one of our guests, I should like to know about
it."

He looked up, and although his smile seemed genuine,
Cecily fancied she saw a watchful look in his eyes. "Nothing
to worry about, Mrs. Sinclair. I was trying to avoid Colonel
Fortescue, that's all. The old boy is harmless enough, but he
can be deadly boring at times. All those endless war stories,
you know."

"Yes, I'm afraid the colonel does get carried away at
times."

Sid Evans sipped his tea. "Anyway, I happened to see
him heading my way last night, and I darted around the
corner of the building to stay out of sight until he had passed.
That's when Gertie caught my attention."

Remembering what Gertie had said about her encounter

with the salesman, Cecily pursed her lips. "You also met my new gardener, Ross McBride, I believe."

This time Sid Evans's gaze slid away from her. "Yes . . . yes, I did. Seems like a nice chap."

"Very. And very protective."

If he understood the significance of her remark, he gave no sign of it. He merely picked up his cup again and drank some more tea.

"Mr. Evans," Cecily said, deciding to plunge in as usual, "how long were you . . . hiding from the colonel?"

"No more than a minute or two. I'd just popped around the corner when Gertie came out of the kitchen. I'd been talking to the brigadier before that. Had quite a long conversation with him, actually."

Cecily looked at him in surprise. "Brigadier Chatsworth?"

"That's right. Interesting fellow. Does he come down here often?"

She was about to answer him when she saw Pansy hurrying across the floor toward her. Her first thought was that it was news of the search for the prophet. Aware of Pansy's loose tongue, Cecily got up quickly from her chair.

She took Sid Evans by surprise, and he stumbled to his feet.

"Don't get up," she told him. "I must get back to my duties."

Pansy reached the table and curtseyed. "Excuse me, mum—"

Cecily held up her hand. "In just a minute, Pansy." She smiled at Sid Evans, who still looked confused at her hasty departure. "If you'll excuse me, Mr. Evans?"

"Oh, certainly, certainly," he mumbled.

"Come along, then, Pansy." Cecily set off across the floor with Pansy scurrying along behind her. Once outside of the dining room, Cecily paused to look back at her. "Now, what is it, Pansy?"

"It's Mrs. Carter-Holmes, mum. She's in the library waiting for you."

"Oh, piffle. I completely forgot about the committee meeting. Thank you, Pansy."

"Yes, mum."

The girl was about to scuttle off, and Cecily held up her hand. "Just a minute, Pansy."

"Yes, mum?"

The maid look frightened, and Cecily felt sorry for the child. She'd lost all that bravado that had served her so well during her interview a week ago. "Pansy, did you happen to mention the murders to anyone other than the staff yesterday?"

Pansy gave her head a decisive shake. "No, mum, I didn't. Mrs. Chubb told us as how we would lose our jobs if we ever talked about hotel business with anyone what didn't work here."

Cecily frowned. "Are you sure?"

Pansy drew her thumb twice across her chest. "Cross me heart, mum. I swear it."

"Very well, Pansy. Thank you."

The girl slipped away, and Cecily thoughtfully watched her go. Her staff had always been extremely loyal. Never had she known word to slip out about hotel matters. The Pennyfoot's unique reputation depended on it, as did the positions of the staff. They were all well aware that a single indiscretion could mean instant dismissal.

Only someone new to the staff would have made such a slip. Yet two of the three new maids were dead at the time the news was leaked, and the third maid swore she hadn't been responsible. Cecily was inclined to believe her. Which could only mean that Sid Evans had lied. The question was, why would he lie? Even more importantly, how did he know about the murders if Pansy hadn't told him about them?

Walking slowly toward the library, Cecily tried to convince herself that it could have been one of the other maids.

Gertie, perhaps, upset over the deaths, could have blurted it out.

She should have asked Sid Evans to whom the maid had been talking at the time, she thought as she reached the door. She should also have a word with Brigadier Chatsworth. Just in case the prophet turned out to be innocent.

For if that were the case, then suspicion was bound to fall onto one of the guests. If the brigadier confirmed that he was talking to Sid Evans at great length during the time of the murder, that would supply them both with an alibi.

Cecily's stomach tightened with anxiety. One of the murders had taken place in a bathroom during the early hours of the morning. The other had occurred in the cellars in the early evening. If the culprit wasn't discovered soon, there could be a third murder. The victim could be anyone in the hotel. They just had to find that prophet soon.

She paused to take a deep, settling breath, then opened the door of the library and walked in.

"Well, I was beginning to worry about you," Phoebe said, smoothing down her elbow-length shell-pink gloves. "What with all these dreadful murders happening, one never knows what to expect next."

Cecily stared at her in dismay. "How did you learn about them?"

"Colonel Fortescue, of course. I met him as I came into the lobby. Quite excited, he was, I must say."

Cecily sat down at the table, feeling more dejected than ever. If Colonel Fortescue had heard, then Sid Evans was right. By now the news was all over the hotel. Which did not bode well for the Pennyfoot's beleaguered reputation.

CHAPTER

❧ 12 ❧

"I really don't know what the world is coming to," Phoebe declared, "what with all this horrendous crime taking place nowadays. Those two young girls, struck down before their prime . . . what a dreadful waste, that's what I say."

"It is a tragedy," Cecily agreed. "Now, about the ball tonight—"

"You are still planning to go ahead with it, then?"

"Of course. The hotel has a tradition to upkeep. We have had a Grand Ball for our season opening ever since the Pennyfoot first opened its door to the public. I see no reason to disappoint our guests this year. Even if there aren't as many visitors as usual."

"Has the murderer been found yet?"

"Not yet, Phoebe, but I'm sure it will be just a matter of time before he is apprehended."

"I certainly hope so. One feels so threatened with someone like that on the loose. The poor colonel is quite shaken, you know. He keeps muttering about standing guard over me with his sword.''

Cecily smiled. ''That's rather gallant of him.''

Phoebe waved an impatient hand in the air. ''Can you just imagine him following me around everywhere brandishing a sword? Quite ridiculous, of course. I should be the laughing stock of the hotel.''

''I think the colonel is very fond of you, Phoebe, in his way.''

To Cecily's surprise, Phoebe actually blushed. She looked down at her silk skirt and plucked at the folds. ''Yes, well . . . as a matter of fact . . .''

Her interest caught, Cecily leaned her elbows on the table and studied her friend. ''Phoebe, whatever are you trying not to tell me?''

''Well, as a matter of fact . . . Oh, bosh, I might as well tell you, but please don't breathe a word to anyone else. Especially Madeline. You know how she is . . .''

''I won't tell Madeline or anyone else,'' Cecily promised, wondering what on earth the secret could be.

''Where is Madeline, anyway?'' Phoebe glanced at the clock. ''She is really late this time.''

''Oh, she won't be here for the meeting. She's coming in this afternoon to set up the flowers and decorations for the ball.''

Phoebe looked relieved. She leaned forward and whispered, ''Colonel Fortescue has asked for my hand in marriage.''

''Good heavens!'' Cecily exclaimed, truly astonished. ''It must be infectious.''

''Really?'' Phoebe's eyes sparkled with curiosity. ''Who else is contemplating marriage, may I ask?''

Annoyed with her slip, Cecily said airily, ''Oh, just a member of my staff. She hasn't given her answer yet, so I'm not at liberty to say her name, but rest assured you will know as soon as it is official.''

"Oh, one of your maids, I suppose." By the look on her face, Phoebe had obviously lost interest.

"So tell me, when is the wedding?"

"Wedding?" Phoebe shook her head. "I'm not going to marry the colonel, Cecily. I admit I had thought about it now and again. All in all, Colonel Fortescue would not be a bad catch, in spite of his rather strange ways. Actually, I think the poor man needs someone to look after him. I, on the other hand, need someone a bit more . . . sophisticated. Such as that quite charming brigadier I met yesterday."

"Brigadier Chatsworth?" Cecily almost laughed out loud. "From what I've heard, the brigadier is a carbon copy of Colonel Fortescue."

"He is rather. In looks, anyway. But I can assure you, Cecily, the brigadier is much more . . . intellectual."

"Really. I had no idea you knew him that well."

"My dear, I hardly spoke to the man. One can tell, however, just from looking at him. Such intelligent eyes."

"And smooth tongue, no doubt," Cecily murmured, still highly amused by Phoebe's fascination with the gentleman.

Phoebe uttered a girlish sigh and patted the wide brim of her hat. "He was rather complimentary," she murmured.

"I thought so."

"Have you met him?"

"No." Cecily glanced at the clock on the wall. "I plan to take care of that omission just as soon as we are finished here."

"Well, I won't detain you." Phoebe folded her gloved hands together and placed them on the table. "My girls are ready with their tableau for tonight. As I mentioned last week, we will be creating a scene from Ancient Greece. Togas and laurel wreaths, my dear. Absolutely stunning, I can promise you. I just hope the little horrors can keep still long enough to accomplish the full effect."

Knowing how much trouble Phoebe's unruly dance troupe usually caused, Cecily fervently echoed that hope. "Well, I'm sure I can leave things in your capable hands," she said, certain of no such thing. Phoebe's presentations had an uncanny way of turning into disaster. Maybe tonight's effort would be the exception.

"Thank you, my dear. I appreciate your confidence in me." Phoebe got fussily to her feet in a rustle of silk taffeta. "I shall be here with my girls, bright and early for the performance tonight."

"I'm looking forward to it," Cecily told her, "and so, I'm sure, are every one of my guests."

Obviously pleased by the comment, Phoebe swept majestically from the room, leaving behind a faint waft of rose water.

Cecily sat for a moment at the table, enjoying the brief respite before she went in search of the brigadier. She was not allowed to enjoy her seclusion for long; a light tap at the door announced the arrival of P.C. Northcott and Inspector Cranshaw.

The inspector strode into the library, barely acknowledging her greeting. A tall, thin man, his face wore a perpetual scowl beneath straight dark brows that were, more often than not, drawn together above his sharp nose.

Behind him, P.C. Northcott's short, chubby figure looked even more dumpy by comparison. He stood by the fireplace, waiting in respectful silence, his pencil poised over the inevitable notepad while his tongue flicked in and out in anticipation of licking the lead point.

"My constable informs me that both young women were strangled by their own stocking," Cranshaw said, coming to an abrupt halt in front of the French windows.

"So I believe," Cecily said evenly. She wished she could have sent for Baxter to stand by her side, but he was somewhere out on the grounds searching for a possible murderer. She crossed her fingers behind her back and willed him to find the man soon.

"I have also been informed that both of the victims were naked and had one shoe missing."

Cecily flinched but managed to answer in a matter-of-fact voice, "That appears to be the case, yes."

"Do you happen to have any insight as to why the shoes are missing?"

"None at all." She looked him straight in the eye. "I am as puzzled by that as you are."

"I see." He apparently did not like the insinuation that he was baffled. "When did you last see the girls?"

"I last saw Flora when she arrived at the hotel two days ago. The three new maids arrived together. They began work that afternoon, and I didn't see Flora again until she was discovered in the bathroom. I spoke to Emily yesterday morning."

"Did she give you any indication that she had seen anything unusual?"

So he'd formed the same theory she had, Cecily thought. He suspected that Emily had seen something incriminating and had been silenced before she could tell anyone. But then she actually *had* seen someone . . . the mad prophet.

For agonizing seconds Cecily fought with her conscience, while the inspector eyed her with suspicion. Finally she said quietly, "As far as I know, Emily saw nothing that could cast light on the mystery."

A half truth at best. But she was reluctant to mention the prophet, at least until he had been found. The last thing she needed was half the constabulary of Badgers End combing through the hotel rooms looking for a man who could well be innocent of any real wrongdoing.

She glanced across at Northcott scribbling laboriously in his notepad before asking, "I assume you will want to question my staff?"

"And your guests." Cranshaw pulled a pocket watch from his vest pocket and examined it. "I don't have the time at present, however. I have to leave on the midday train for London, where I have urgent business. I plan on returning on the late train tonight, and I will be here at the hotel early in the morning. P.C. Northcott will remain here in order to make certain that no one leaves the hotel before I've had a chance to interview them.''

Cecily closed her eyes in a brief gesture of dismay. It was worse than she thought. Her guests would now be virtual prisoners until the inspector had talked to every one of them. That could take the entire day.

She thought about protesting, but before she could speak, Cranshaw added, ''I must inform you, Mrs. Sinclair, that I can no longer accept the state of affairs in this hotel. A double murder in the space of one day is a serious crime indeed and cannot be ignored.''

''I agree, Inspector,'' Cecily said hastily, ''which is why I have taken the precaution of ordering the closure of the card rooms in the cellar. They will not be opened again for gambling as long as I am the owner of this hotel.''

Cranshaw had the grace to give her a look of approval. ''I am glad to hear it, Mrs. Sinclair. While I sympathize with your position, however, I must take this a step further. If the criminal who did this terrible deed is not apprehended by tomorrow night, I shall have no other recourse than to close the Pennyfoot Hotel down. Permanently.''

She bit back her cry of protest. It was, after all, no more than she had been expecting. It was futile to argue, in any case. She knew, from past experience, that once the inspector handed down a decision, no argument in the world would sway him. Instead, she lifted her chin and met his gaze with a dignified silence.

He appeared to be somewhat taken aback by her acquiescence. He looked at Northcott, who seemed disappointed that the battle he'd been expecting hadn't materialized.

''You will remain here, Constable, until I return,'' Cranshaw ordered. ''Do not let anyone out of this hotel until I give him permission to leave.''

''Yessir!'' The constable nodded, his small beady eyes glistening with excitement.

''As for you, Mrs. Sinclair . . .'' Cranshaw fixed his cold gaze on her face. ''I should not have to remind you of the consequences should you take matters into your own hands.''

Still she met his gaze without flinching. "I'll bear it in mind, Inspector."

His face darkened for an instant, then with a curt nod he spun on his heel and marched from the room.

"Whew!" Northcott wiped his forehead with the back of his sleeve. "That were a close one."

"I will have a chair and table set up for you in the lobby, Constable," Cecily said, crossing to the door which now stood ajar. "I assume you will want to take your meals there?"

Northcott was already licking his lips in anticipation. "That will do very well. Yes, thank you, Mrs. Sinclair."

"Not at all, Constable. If you would care to wait here a few moments longer, I will send one of the maids to inform you when it is ready."

"Yes, mum. Much obliged, I'm sure."

She left him standing by the fireplace with his mouth visibly watering. If there was one thing P.C. Northcott loved above all else, it was Michel's cooking and Mrs. Chubb's baking. A generous tray of food should keep him occupied for a while, and in the meantime, she would hunt down Brigadier Chatsworth and find out if Sid Evans was telling the truth when he said he'd been chatting to that gentleman while the second murder was taking place.

After visiting the drawing room and the bar without encountering the brigadier, Cecily played a hunch and headed for the bowling green. Chatsworth was there, entertaining a group of fascinated ladies while showing off his prowess with the heavy wooden ball.

Cecily recognized him immediately . . . a portly gentleman with ruddy cheeks, thick white hair, and bushy whiskers. She watched him roll the ball expertly across the smooth lawn to rest in an excellent position within the circle. Squeals of delight and polite clapping greeted his effort.

Deciding to wait until the game was finished, Cecily retreated to the rose arbor, from where she could see a portion of the bowling green. Seated in the warm sunshine, she was glad of the wide-brimmed straw hat she'd donned before venturing outdoors.

She had barely begun to relax when Baxter's tall figure appeared at the other end of the rose garden. Catching sight of her, he strode purposefully toward her, while she waited in breathless anxiety for him to reach her.

"Tell me," she commanded as soon as he was close enough to hear her. "What has happened? Did you find him?"

Baxter's face was grave as he shook his head. "I'm sorry, Cecily. There has been no sign of him since Daisy saw him this morning. If he is still on the grounds, he has found a hiding place of which I'm not aware. We have searched the entire place, inside and out."

"Then he must have left." She didn't know how to feel about that. His presence on the hotel grounds was a constant source of fear, yet if he had decided to leave he would vanish altogether, and there would be little chance of finding him. Especially by tomorrow night.

She looked up at Baxter, who immediately dropped onto the bench beside her.

"What is it, Cecily? Has something else happened?"

"Inspector Cranshaw," Cecily answered gloomily. She quickly repeated the inspector's words as Baxter's face grew more and more grave. "I suppose it was no more than to be expected," she said when she'd finished. "He really has been remarkably tolerant up until now."

"For the sake of the aristocracy, that was all." Baxter shook his head. "He was afraid to risk incurring their wrath. Now that we have very few noblemen visiting the Pennyfoot, he can afford to put his foot down."

"Well, we shall simply have to renew our efforts to find this man, that's all." Cecily thought for a moment. "Where is Samuel?"

"He's on the roof, inspecting the chimneys. I sent him up

there as soon as we finished searching the hotel.''

Cecily nodded. ''As soon as he comes down, have him go into Badgers End and search the town. Perhaps he'll catch sight of the prophet there.''

''Very well. I'll call the railway station as well. I'll give the stationmaster a description. He might be able to tell me if the man boarded the early train to London.''

''He might even get on the midday one, in which case he'll be traveling on the same train as the inspector.'' Cecily sighed. ''Wouldn't that be ironic.''

Baxter leaned his arm around her shoulders. ''Try not to worry, Cecily. I know things look black, but they've looked black before, and we've managed to survive them all.''

''That was when we could rely on the inspector to turn a blind eye, in spite of his constant warnings.'' She leaned against his warm strength, attempting to draw courage from his comforting presence. ''I'm afraid, Baxter, that this time we shall not be so fortunate.''

He was silent for so long she was reluctant to look at him, for fear his expression would mirror her own anxiety. Then he said quietly, ''If that happens . . . if the hotel is shut down for good, we shall simply have to start again somewhere else.''

She shook her head, fighting back a tear. ''No, I'm too old to start again. Too tired, too beaten, too dispirited.''

''To borrow one of your fondest phrases, my dear . . . pif-fle. You will never be too old to try anything new. You are much too strong-spirited, iron-willed, and invincible. You will rise again to conquer new worlds, and together we shall endure.''

She peeked up at him. ''You make me sound like one of those decrepit old ships languishing in dry dock.''

His shout of laughter cheered her to no end. ''Cecily, my dearest, you are an absolute delight. However would I live this life without you?''

''I hope you never have to, Baxter. Nor I without you.''

"Perhaps I should choose this moment to propose marriage."

"No, you are right." She smiled at him fondly, grateful for his love. "It should be a very special moment, captured for all eternity. We will wait until we can have the privacy and peace to do things properly."

He smiled down at her. "Am I really such a bore?"

"Not at all. I wouldn't have you any other way." She gave him an impish grin. "If I tell you a secret, will you promise not to repeat it?"

"Of course."

"Colonel Fortescue has asked Phoebe for her hand."

"Good Lord." He was silent for a moment. "Has she accepted?"

"Not yet. I think she's waiting to see how things transpire between her and Brigadier Chatsworth."

Baxter's jaw dropped. "You can't be serious."

"Perfectly."

He shook his head in amazement. "I must confess I find it difficult to picture Phoebe enamored with either one of them."

"That isn't all. Ross McBride has asked for Gertie's hand. I do believe, dear Baxter, that we have started an epidemic."

He looked stunned for a moment, and then he smiled. "All I can say to that, my dear madam, is that there couldn't be a more pleasant epidemic in existence. All that is left is for our good Dr. Prestwick to cease playing the social butterfly and settle for one woman, and I shall be convinced that we have indeed infected the entire population with our joy."

A sudden memory of Madeline's flushed face made Cecily smile as well. "Stranger things have happened," she murmured. "You just never know what might be around the next corner."

CHAPTER

❦ 13 ❦

A burst of applause caught Cecily's attention, and she glanced over at the bowling green. "The game is finished," she said, rising to her feet. "I want a word with Brigadier Chatsworth."

Baxter looked surprised. "Is there a problem?"

"Not as far as I'm aware." She smiled up at him. "I'll tell you all about it later. Unless you want to come with me?"

He shook his head, though he looked a trifle concerned. "I must take care of the luncheon arrangements. The tables will have to be cleared promptly in order to prepare the ballroom for the ball tonight."

"Very well, I'll catch up with you later." She patted his arm. "Please don't worry, Baxter. I have no intention of stepping on the inspector's toes."

Baxter's expression changed. "We'll have him to deal with in the morning, I suppose."

She nodded. "I almost forgot to tell you. P.C. Northcott has been posted on guard, to make sure no one leaves without being questioned tomorrow."

"What?" Baxter ran a hand through his hair. "That's all we needed," he muttered.

"I've arranged to have a table set up in the lobby." Seeing Baxter's aghast look, she added quickly, "As inconspicuously as possible, of course. I thought it was the best place. I suppose we shall have to make some sort of announcement at the ball tonight."

"I suppose you're right." He sighed and lifted his face to the sky. "There are times when I wonder if this hotel is cursed. Perhaps you should ask Madeline to look into it. Maybe she can do something to get rid of it." His expression suggested he was only half joking.

Personally Cecily thought that might not be a bad idea. Just then Chatsworth's rotund figure sauntered across the lawns, and with a hurried promise to Baxter to meet him in his office later, Cecily hurriedly left the rose garden to waylay the brigadier.

She caught up with him just before he reached the steps to the hotel lobby. "Brigadier!" she exclaimed, raising her voice in order to get his attention. "What a splendid game of bowls you play!"

Chatsworth drew to a halt, looking very pleased with himself. Straightening his tie with both hands, he murmured, "I had no idea you were watching the contest, Mrs. Sinclair."

"Oh, indeed I was. From the rose garden." She waved a vague hand in that direction. "You are to be congratulated, sir."

"Thank you, madam." He inclined his head. "I do enjoy the game."

"So I perceive." She looked around the gardens as if searching for someone. "You haven't seen Mr. Evans, have you? I wanted a word with him, but I don't see him about anywhere."

"Probably in his room, I should think." The brigadier twirled his mustache. "Must be nearly time for the luncheon."

"In a few minutes, yes."

"Thought so. The old tummy rumbling, you know. Knows the time better than I do, what?"

"Quite." Determined not to be put off, Cecily said quite casually, "Mr. Evans told me he had a very pleasant conversation with you yesterday evening."

The brigadier appeared to go strangely still, and his eyes beneath the bushy white brows seemed sharper than she remembered. "Really. Well, I enjoyed it, too. As a matter of fact, we shared a couple of drinks together in the bar. Nice chap. Has some interesting stories to tell."

Cecily wouldn't have thought that the brigadier would have been interested in anything Sid Evans had to say. The two men were obviously from very different walks of life, and the two didn't often mix. Her theory that Sid Evans had been lying was obviously unfounded, however.

Feeling somewhat deflated, Cecily changed the subject. "I trust you will be attending the ball this evening?"

"Of course! Wouldn't miss it, dear lady. I'm told that Mrs. Carter-Holmes's presentations are quite spectacular."

Sometimes considerably more so than Phoebe anticipated, Cecily thought wryly. "Indeed. Where did you hear that?"

"Colonel Fortescue. He seems to be quite enamored of the lady."

"So I understand. Mrs. Carter-Holmes is a very gracious lady. I can understand why he admires her. I do believe his regard for her is quite genuine." She gave the brigadier a straight look. "I should hate to think that anyone would toy with the lady's affections."

"I agree, madam. That would be most despicable."

His expression remained perfectly innocent, and Cecily had to be content with that. After all, Phoebe's affairs were none of her business, she told herself as she hurried up the steps a minute or two later. Though she rather hoped that her friend wouldn't take the brigadier too seriously.

Although he seemed pleasant enough and was certainly respectful, Cecily couldn't quite dismiss the feeling that behind that roguish face and charming smile there lurked a man who intensely disliked being crossed. Something told her that Brigadier Chatsworth could have a formidable temper if provoked.

"I looked all over the town," Samuel told Cecily later that afternoon when she admitted him to the library. "I didn't see no sign of him, but I did go into Dolly's tea shop to ask her if she'd seen him about." Samuel paused, as if making the most of a dramatic situation. "She said she'd seen him a few days ago."

"Really?" Cecily closed the file she was working on and stared up at Samuel. "Did she say anything else about him?"

"Just that he'd gone around the tables telling everyone the world was going to end. Dolly threw him out."

Cecily smiled. Since Dolly probably outweighed the man by a stone or two, she was more than capable of managing that feat. "She hasn't seen him since?"

"No, mum. Nor has anyone else."

"All right, Samuel. Thank you." Cecily looked up as he reached the door. "I don't suppose you found anything in the chimneys?"

"Not even a feather, mum. Either Sid Evans was hearing things, or whatever it was flew away."

"Well, at least we won't have to worry about the next occupant of that room."

Cecily glanced up at the clock as Samuel closed the door behind him. Madeline should be finished setting up the flowers and decorations for the ball by now. Phoebe would be arriving soon with her chattering group of wayward dancers, ahead of the musicians who would accompany the tableau.

It was time to return to her suite to dress for the occasion.

She had just reached the door when it opened abruptly, and Madeline stood on the threshold. "I've completed the decorating," she announced as Cecily moved back into the room. "I think you'll like the effect."

"You always do such a wonderful job," Cecily assured her friend sincerely. "The ball would not be the same without your exquisite touch."

Madeline smiled, though her face looked rather strained. "I was just wondering if Dr. Prestwick would be at the ball tonight," she said casually. "I would like to ask his opinion on something, and I really don't want to go down to that dreadful surgery of his. It's always full of women preening and cooing, making general fools of themselves."

"He has been invited, as usual. He doesn't usually come, but then one never knows."

"Well, I suppose I shall simply have to wait and see."

"You could always give him a ring on the telephone if it's urgent."

Madeline shook her head. "I don't trust these newfangled machines. One never knows who might be listening to your private conversation."

Cecily wondered what Madeline had to ask Kevin Prestwick that was so private. Surely her friend wasn't ill? She did look rather peaked, now that she came to think about it. Alarmed now, Cecily asked urgently, "Is something wrong, Madeline? Are you not well?"

Madeline shook her head in a rather vague way. "I feel perfectly well, thank you, Cecily. Except . . ."

Her voice trailed off, increasing Cecily's concern. "What is it, Madeline? Please tell me."

Madeline gave her a troubled look. "I know this is silly, but . . ."

"Yes? What is it?"

"It's just that I have the very odd feeling that this is the last time I shall be decorating the ballroom for you, that's all."

Shocked, Cecily stared at her friend. "Whatever do you mean?"

"Oh, I don't know." Madeline shrugged her slim shoulders. "You know how I get these feelings. More often than not they mean nothing. Don't worry, Cecily. I'll see you at the ball."

She drifted out the door and disappeared. Cecily stared after her, disturbed by her words. *You know how I get these feelings. More often than not they mean nothing.* But Cecily knew just the opposite. More often than not, Madeline's predictions bore fruit.

Her words could mean anything. It could be that Madeline would do something else with her life. On the other hand, this could well be the last ball ever held at the Pennyfoot. All Cecily could hope and pray for was that Madeline's prediction didn't mean that something terrible was about to happen to her.

Phoebe winced as she made her way to the dressing rooms backstage. She could hear the commotion long before she drew close to the door. Someone, or something, had obviously upset her dance troupe. Not that it took much to throw those dreadful girls into total bedlam, of course. If it didn't happen at least once during final rehearsal, Phoebe would have been seriously concerned.

As it was, things were comparatively normal when she threw open the door. The dancers were all partially dressed. Costumes and accessories were strewn everywhere, hanging from the back of chairs, crumpled on the floor, flung across the screens or, in one particularly horrific instance, draped seductively over a portrait of the new king.

Utter sacrilege, Phoebe thought, snatching down the offending petticoat. She could scarcely think with all the racket going on.

Marion's harsh voice seemed the loudest, strident above the high-pitched nattering of Isabelle who was doing her best to comfort Dora who, in turn, seemed to be in the final throes of an hysterical fit.

Phoebe drew her hourglass figure up to her full height, which was still considerably less than most of her charges, and yelled at the top of her voice, "Quiet!"

No one took the slightest bit of notice of her, of course. Highly irritated, Phoebe clapped her hands and yelled again. "I . . . said . . . *quiet!*"

She managed to catch Marion's eye, but the despicable child simply went on mouthing something unintelligible in that awful, sergeant-major voice of hers, while Dora howled louder.

Deciding to get to the heart of the trouble, Phoebe shoved her way through the fascinated group of girls, all of whom seemed to be trying to outdo each other with raised voices.

Dora stood huddled in the middle of the circle with her mouth wide open, emitting the most ghastly wails Phoebe had ever heard. She took one look, sized up the situation, made her decision, lifted her hand, and gave the girl a hearty whack across the cheek.

The wails mercifully stopped. For a second or two, anyway, as Dora stared at her assailant in shocked disbelief. Then she opened her mouth and let out an even louder shriek. "You hit me! I'm going to tell my mum you flipping hit me!"

"Of course I hit you," Phoebe said crossly. "It is the recognized method to cure hysteria, as you very well know, and I shall have no hesitation in hitting you again if you don't stop that horrendous noise this instant."

She raised her hand, and Dora snapped her mouth shut. For one blissful second there was silence, then the girls all started talking at once.

Three times Phoebe called for silence. The dancers were talking too loud to hear her, or more likely, they were determined to ignore her. Having reached the end of her tether, Phoebe lifted her hand, took hold of Marion's ear and gave it a sharp tug.

"Ow!" Marion yelled. "You're hurting me!"

"I'll hurt you even more," Phoebe shouted, "if you don't use your dubious influence and quieten this rabble at once!"

Marion obediently opened her mouth and bellowed, "Shut up and pipe down, you bleeding lot!"

Like magic, the girls simmered down, until just a whisper or two escaped from their quivering lips.

"Now," Phoebe said, feeling quite breathless, "please be so kind as to enlighten me of the cause of this disgusting display."

"It were Dora, Mrs. Carter-Holmes," Isabelle said, pointing at the shivering girl in the center of attention. "She thinks the world is coming to an end."

The dancers began nervously chattering again, and Phoebe lifted her hand. Marion ducked out of the way, yelling, "It weren't my fault!"

"Quiet!" Phoebe screeched.

This time the girls quietened down to a resentful murmur.

Unfortunately someone chose that precise moment to bang loudly on the door, starting up Dora's wails again. "Oo, it's 'im. I know it's 'im."

Whoever "him" was, Phoebe had no idea, but she was determined to find out who had upset her girls in such a way. Amid screams of warning, she marched to the door and flung it open, completely forgetting that her girls were indecently exposed in their underwear.

Their ear-splitting shrieks reminded her in a hurry, however, and she slipped through the door and closed it behind her. Confronting the tall gentleman standing in the narrow passageway, she made an effort to compose herself. She could only hope he hadn't heard her shrieking at those miserable fiends.

She softened her voice, moistened her lips, and murmured coyly, "Mr. Sandringham. What brings you backstage?"

Edward Sandringham waved an elegant hand at the door. "I heard the commotion and I wondered if I might be of some assistance."

"Oh, how terribly kind." Phoebe fluttered her eyelashes. "But I do assure you I have things completely under control." Which wasn't strictly the truth, as she was painfully aware, judging from the wailing beginning to rise behind the closed door once more.

Edward Sandringham sent a wary glance at the door, but happily he seemed to accept her word that all was well. "In any case, Mrs. Carter-Holmes, I'm pleased to have the chance to speak to you again."

"Oh, well—" Phoebe wished she had a fan behind which she could hide her warm cheeks. "That's most kind of you, Mr. Sandringham."

"I understand that you are . . . ah . . . responsible for the events at the hotel?"

Phoebe wasn't sure she liked the way he'd phrased that, but his face looked perfectly innocent, so she could afford to give him the benefit of the doubt. Preening just a little, she said modestly, "I organize the entertainment, yes. I try to create an extravaganza fitting for such a prestigious hotel."

Sandringham nodded. "Quite, quite. I'm sure you do an admirable job. Do you find it difficult to locate new and interesting talent in the vicinity, or do you rely mostly on a regular group of local artistes?"

Phoebe frowned. Not sure what this had to do with anything, she answered carefully, "Badgers End is a small village, Mr. Sandringham. We look for our entertainers in various places. Wellercombe, mostly, though we have prevailed at times upon the talents of some of our more celebrated guests."

"I see. Do you get a lot of theatrical people staying at the Pennyfoot?"

He was beginning to make her feel most uncomfortable. No one had ever asked her these kinds of questions before. Somehow she had the feeling his interest went beyond mild curiosity. Deciding that she'd said quite enough, she said just a little brusquely, "I hope you will forgive me, sir, but I must get back to my dance troupe."

As if in answer to her words, a chorus of wails echoed down the passageway.

Sandringham sent a harried look at the closed door. "Well, if you're sure I can't be of help—"

"Thank you, Mr. Sandringham. I trust you will enjoy our little tableau."

"I'm sure I shall." He swept her a bow, then strode off down the passageway, his broad shoulders making the space seem narrower than she ever remembered.

She would have liked to stay and ponder on his words, but the level of noise from inside the dressing room was once more reaching unacceptable heights.

Phoebe flung open the door and strutted in like an enraged cockerel. "Will you *please* be *quiet*!"

"Strewth!" Marion muttered, just happening to be closest to the door at that moment. "You scared me to bloody bits."

Ignoring her, Phoebe plunged once more into the center of the wailing girls. This time she didn't waste her breath. Instead, she raised her hand, twirled around, and managed to slap every face within reach in one fell blow.

Order was restored almost immediately.

"Now," Phoebe said, panting for breath, "I would like Dora to tell me why she thinks the world is coming to an end."

"He told me it was," Dora said, her voice trembling pitiably. "He told me we was all supposed to prepare for the end."

A series of hollow moans greeted this statement.

Phoebe thrust her hand in the air, miraculously achieving silence again. "Who is this 'he'?" she demanded.

Dora shook her head, apparently unable to bring herself to say the words.

"Will somebody please tell me?" Phoebe jutted her chin at a dangerous angle.

Marion must have recognized the danger signals. "You know what a twit Dora is," she said in her belligerent voice. "She'll believe anything. He was just having a bit of fun, that's all."

"No, he weren't," Dora burst out, recovering her voice. "He had weird eyes, he did. Like Jack the Ripper."

Isabelle uttered a shrill scream that cut off when Phoebe glared at her.

"Where was this man?" she demanded, beginning to feel a little nervous herself. She didn't think the girls had heard about the murders yet, or they surely would have mentioned it by now. Whoever this man was, however, it seemed that he had badly frightened Dora.

"He was upstairs in the hallway," Dora muttered. "I seen him when I came in."

"Did you see where he went?"

Dora shook her head. "No, I was too frightened to watch where he went. I ran away from him. Oh, Mrs. Carter-Holmes, you don't think the world is coming to an end, do you?"

The wails started again, and Phoebe lifted both her hands. "Of course the world isn't coming to an end," she declared when it was quiet once more. "That is a lot of nonsense, and whoever is spreading such a ridiculous rumor around is disturbed in his mind. Just forget about it."

"We don't have to get prepared?" Dora asked in a quavering voice.

"The only thing you have to get prepared for right now," Phoebe said grimly, "is this tableau, which I still have fond hopes of presenting tonight. You have exactly ten minutes to get dressed. I don't want to hear another word about the world coming to an end."

Their mumbled chorus of, "Yes, Mrs. Carter-Holmes," was uttered in unison.

She'd managed to reassure the dancers, Phoebe thought as they scurried about the room, but she was none too convinced herself. The very first opportunity she got, she decided, she would tell Cecily or Baxter about the man with strange eyes who insisted the world was coming to an end.

And heaven help them all if he was right.

CHAPTER
❀ 14 ❀

Mrs. Chubb looked up at the mantelpiece clock and uttered a yelp of dismay. "Just look at the time! Where is that Samuel? He was supposed to be here fifteen minutes ago."

"I know where he is," Gertie muttered. She lifted the ladle from a jug of cream and poured the thick mixture into the silver jugs which sat on a tray in front of her. "He went to help Mr. Baxter."

"Well, I wish he'd get back here," Mrs. Chubb said crossly. "I need Samuel here in the kitchen. We're never going to get this kitchen cleaned up if we don't have some help."

"Comes to something," Gertie grumbled, "when the bleeding stable manager has to help in the kitchen."

"Everyone has had to do extra since those poor girls died." The housekeeper slapped her hand down on a hapless fly, then flicked the dead bug off the table. "Samuel understands that, and he doesn't complain."

Meaning she did, Gertie thought, feeling resentful. After all, she'd been the one who'd taken on most of the bloody extra work. Nearly dead on her flipping feet, she was. Not that any bleeding one would notice.

"Pansy, Madam wants these clean towels to go up to the second-floor bathroom," the housekeeper ordered. "I was going to ask Samuel, but since he's not here, you'll have to take them."

"All by meself?" Pansy's face looked pinched with fright. "I'm not going up in those dark hallways all by meself at night with that murderer walking around."

"Don't be silly, child. This hotel has been searched from top to bottom, and there was no sign of that man. Samuel told me himself."

"I don't want to go up there!" Pansy wailed. "Why can't Gertie go?"

Gertie opened her mouth to protest, but Mrs. Chubb forestalled her. "Gertie can't go because she has to go in and clear the tables, that's why."

Gertie's chin shot up. "Who me?"

"Just as soon as you've finished those creamers," Mrs. Chubb said firmly.

"It's not my bleeding job to clear the tables." Gertie glared at Pansy. "It's her bloody job."

"I'll clear the tables." Pansy looked hopefully at the housekeeper. "I don't mind, Mrs. Chubb, honest. Then Gertie can take the towels up."

"Strewth!" Gertie dumped the ladle into the cream so hard the mixture slurped over the side. "Now look what you bleeding made me do."

"Gertie will clear the tables," Mrs. Chubb said in her you'd-better-do-what-I-say voice. "She's quicker than you, Pansy. You take these towels up and be quick about it. Then come straight back here. We'll all be here until the morning if we don't all get a move on."

Pansy looked as if she were about to be sick, but she took the towels and dragged her feet over to the door, looking back over her shoulder when she reached it. "What if I see Samuel on the way?"

"Don't waste time looking for him, take them up yourself. And get a move on!"

Mrs. Chubb's raised voice had the desired effect. Pansy scuttled through the door, allowing it to swing to behind her.

"I'll take those creamers out to the dining room, Gertie." The housekeeper picked the tray up off the table. "You get the trolley and go clear those dishes. You know how Mr. Baxter hates to have them sitting on the tables too long, and the tableau will be starting soon."

"Oh, all bleeding right." Gertie dragged off her apron, then straightened her cap. "I'll be glad when Madam gets some new staff. I might as well be bleeding married, all the work I do around here."

"You'll work a darn sight harder in your own home." Carrying the tray of creamers, Mrs. Chubb hurried to the door and jerked it open with her hip. "Especially with those two little ones running around."

"Yeah, but I'll bleeding have something to look forward to at the end of the day." Gertie winked, enjoying the flustered look Mrs. Chubb shot at her.

"Gertie Brown! What a thing to say!"

Gertie shrugged, doing her best to look innocent. "I was only talking about having dinner with me flipping husband. What's bleeding wrong about that?"

To her intense satisfaction, the housekeeper's face turned red. She made an explosive sound in her throat, then barged through the door. Gertie could hear the creamers rattling all the way up the steps.

Serve her bleeding well right, she thought, dragging the trolley out of the pantry. Mrs. Chubb was beginning to get on her nerves. They never had laughs like they used to in the old days when Ethel worked there and both Doris and Daisy were in the kitchen.

Now there was just her and Pansy, with Samuel getting in the way more than helping. Things were really getting bad at the Pennyfoot.

Pulling the trolley behind her, she trudged up the steps to the foyer. The wheels rattled on the parquet floor, disturbing Constable Northcott, who had been dozing at his table in a dark corner.

"What time is it?" he demanded, peering sleepily at the face of the grandfather clock.

"Almost ten, sir," Gertie said, bouncing the trolley to make it sound louder. The old fool was supposed to be on duty, not snoring his head off so loud she could hear him in the kitchen.

"Ah, yes." The constable settled himself down again, his chin resting on his chest.

Gertie sighed and dragged the trolley down the hall to the dining room. She could hear the musicians tuning up. She had to hurry if she was going to get the bloody dishes off the tables before the tableau.

Head down, she charged along the hallway, skidded around the corner, and ran full tilt into a tall, well-dressed gentleman coming in the opposite direction.

"Ooh, bloody hell," she muttered before she could stop the words from spilling out. "Sorry, sir. I didn't expect no one to be here."

"Quite all right." The gentleman peered closer at her in the flickering shadows from the gas lamps. "Gertie, isn't it?"

She looked up in surprise, wondering how he knew her name. "Yes, sir. I'm sorry, sir, I don't—"

"Edward Sandringham. I wonder if you'd mind answering a question for me?"

"Certainly, sir." The orchestra struck up the opening chords, and Gertie looked anxiously down the hall. "I don't have much time right now, though."

"Oh, this won't take a minute. I just wanted to know where the hotel staff buy the vegetables and fruit."

Taken aback by the question, Gertie had to think. "Well, we buys it from the farms, mostly. When John Thimble was a gardener here, we grew a lot of it. Still do grow some, but the rest we get from the farms."

"I see. What about meat and poultry?"

"Abbitson's, the butchers in the High Street."

"And bread? Flour?"

"The mill. Mrs. Chubb makes all the bread. And the pastries. Though sometimes we get them from Dolly's tea shop in the village." She was beginning to feel uneasy about all these bloody questions. "Look," she said, taking care to keep the trolley between them, "I do have to get to the dining room. If I don't get those bleeding tables cleared, Mrs. Chubb will have me blinking guts for garters, that she will."

Edward Sandringham laughed, the kind of a soft sound that gave women shivery skin. "Go on with you, then," he said and strode off to the foyer.

Ross laughed like that, Gertie thought, as she hurried down the hall, only he made her feel a lot more than shivery skin. He made her feel what no one had ever done before. She couldn't stop thinking about him lately. In fact, every minute she spent away from him seemed like a year.

She felt a sudden deep longing to see him. Just as soon as she got through with the tables, she decided. Before she went back to settle the babies down. What with being so bleeding busy, she hadn't had time to say more'n two words to him. And it was suddenly important to say what was on her mind.

She didn't know when or how it had happened, but now she was sure of what she wanted to do. She'd made up her mind. She'd find Ross and give him her answer, once and for all.

It didn't occur to her until much later to wonder why Edward Sandringham had left the ballroom just when things were starting to get interesting.

• • •

"What do you mean you haven't seen her?" Mrs. Chubb stared at Samuel in dismay. "She's been gone over half an hour. Did you look in the second-floor bathroom like I told you?"

"I told you, I just come from there. I didn't see her." Samuel marched over to the sink to wash his hands. "She must have gone somewhere else."

"She wouldn't have gone anywhere else. I told her to come straight back here."

"Well, maids don't always do what they're told to do." Samuel grabbed a tea towel from the top of the stove and dried his hands. "She'll be back soon, I reckon. Now what do you want me to do?"

"I need those dishes put away in the cupboards," Mrs. Chubb said. "Be careful with them, though. They're the good ones and cost a fortune."

"I never could understand why people spend all that money on plates." Samuel opened the cupboard door and began stacking the dishes inside. "After all, they just get mucked up with food, don't they. I mean, how many people do you think notice the pattern on a plate when they're eating off it?"

Mrs. Chubb nodded absently, though she wasn't really listening. She was remembering Pansy's face and her scared voice. *I'm not going up in those dark hallways at night all by meself with that murderer walking around.*

But she had gone up there. And she hadn't come back. Mrs. Chubb had a nasty sinking feeling in the pit of her stomach. Two girls dead, and now Pansy missing. Hardly aware that her lips were moving, she whispered, "Please, not Pansy. It's all my fault. Please let her be all right."

"What?" Samuel had stopped what he was doing and was staring at her, his eyes suddenly wide with apprehension.

"Samuel," Mrs. Chubb said, her throat suddenly dry. "Go and find Mr. Baxter. As fast as you can."

•   •   •

Cecily made her way across the ballroom, greeting some of the guests as she passed. Dressed in pale lemon chiffon, she felt almost girlish when more than one gentleman complimented her on her gown. The only opinion that truly mattered to her would come from Baxter, however, if he chose to comment at all.

Sometimes, Cecily thought, smiling to herself, words weren't necessary where Baxter was concerned. He was not one to use flowery phrases, except on the most crucial occasions, but his eyes could convey the most wonderful declarations of his regard and admiration. That, as far as she was concerned, was enough. Certainly more than all the effusive compliments handed out by Dr. Prestwick.

Thinking of Dr. Prestwick made her think of Madeline. Cecily glanced up at the balconies as she crossed the sprung, parquet floor. Festoons of yellow, green, and purple ribbons swooped in graceful curves above her head. They framed magnificent bouquets of yellow and pink roses, mingled with fragrant lilac and pink mimosa.

How Madeline loved her flowers. Cecily knew that her friend had ordered them early in the week as usual, and would have risen at dawn that morning to oversee the delivery of the fragile blossoms. Transported by train from Covent Garden, the flowers no doubt had been packed and handled with extreme care.

Madeline had then worked her usual magic with the flowers, creating truly remarkable floral arrangements that seemed to be growing right out of the smiling alabaster cherubs that supported them.

Cecily's smile faded. If Madeline's disturbing prediction were to come true, then she would be sorely missed at the Pennyfoot. Not to mention the entire village of Badgers End.

Madeline's potions, fashioned from wildflowers and herbs, were widely sought after by skeptics who shunned the more modern methods of healing. Even the most sophisticated had tried her remedies at times, and there were many men who swore by her aphrodisiacs, though personally Cecily was inclined to believe that particular remedy lay in the mind rather than in a potion.

There was no doubt that Madeline's absence would be deeply felt by one and all.

Immersed in troubled thoughts about her friend, Cecily failed to see Colonel Fortescue until his harsh voice cut across her musing.

"I say, old bean, you look rather ravishing tonight, what?"

The colonel stood close by the stage, where the musicians were already setting up their instruments. Cecily planned to look in on Phoebe before the dancers were due to perform their tableau. More often than not, Phoebe needed help to subdue those high-spirited young women.

At the sight of the colonel beaming at her, Cecily braced herself. She would just have to be rude if he insisted on keeping her talking.

"Good evening, Colonel. You are looking rather spiffing yourself, if I may say so."

"You may certainly say so, madam. And I thank you, indeed, for the compliment. I just hope Phoebe shares your opinion." He frowned, peering about him in a rather short-sighted way. "I don't suppose you've seen her anywhere around, have you, old bean? I've been standing here for half an hour and haven't seen her yet."

"I'm afraid Phoebe will be quite busy for the next few minutes," Cecily said, edging toward the door that led to the backstage area. "She is preparing her dancers for the tableau that will take place shortly."

"Bless my soul, I clean forgot." The colonel lifted his hand to smite his brow with such force the impact knocked him backwards. He shook his head, eyes watering, while Cecily anxiously watched. After a moment or two he appeared to recover.

"Are you feeling all right, Colonel?" Cecily asked, feeling compelled to make sure before she left him.

"Oh, quite, quite, old girl. What was I saying? Oh, yes,

I was talking about Phoebe. Told me she'd meet me after the show. Stupid of me to forget. The old memory isn't what it used to be, what?''

Cecily smiled. ''It happens to all of us, Colonel. Now, if you'll excuse me—''

''Take that brigadier chap, Chatsby, or Chatsbury—''

''Chatsworth,'' Cecily said, glancing up at the musicians. They were tuning their instruments in soft discordant wails. Any minute now, Phoebe would be lining up her girls. ''Colonel, I'm sorry, I really—''

''Chatsworth, that's it! Strange, that is. He was in Africa same place, same time as I was. Even looks like me.'' He leaned forward, swaying a little on his feet.

Cecily understood the reason for that when she received a blast of his gin-laced breath.

Righting himself, the colonel muttered, ''You don't think he *is* me, do you, old girl?''

Cecily backed away. ''I really don't think you need worry about that, Colonel. You and the brigadier are quite different people, you know.''

''Ah, well, that's a relief. Thought it was my mind going. Can't remember half the stuff he tells me happened in the Boer War. Sometimes I think I'll forget my blasted name. That would never do, what?''

''Certainly not, Colonel. Now if you'll excuse me—'' She broke off as the conductor tapped his baton on the podium. The orchestra struck up the opening chords to a smattering of applause.

There was no point in going backstage to help Phoebe now, Cecily thought, her gaze on the wings. The girls were due to walk on any second, and Phoebe would be out in front of the stage hissing directions at them.

Baxter had promised to join her for the performance, and she was looking forward to spending the time in his company. The colonel had drifted off, no doubt in search of his table.

She took her seat at her own table, just as Baxter appeared

through the main doors. For a little while she could relax and just enjoy being with him, she thought as she watched him approach. Now all she had to hope for was that for once the presentation would not end in disaster.

CHAPTER

❀ 15 ❀

"Now!" Phoebe commanded in a loud whisper as she herded the girls into the wings. "Slowly . . . one at a time, and please pay attention to the person in front of you. Remember, one slip and you all fall down."

"Like London Bridge," Marion commented out of the corner of her mouth.

Isabelle giggled, while someone else hissed, "Sshhhh!"

Phoebe sent up a silent prayer. Not that it did much good, as she knew from past experience, but it didn't do any harm to try.

The girls did look rather fetching in their white togas, she decided, even if their costumes did leave a little too much expanse of skin over the one bared shoulder.

She really would have to have a word with Marion's mother. The woman had been kind enough to offer to make the costumes, apparently under the misconception that her daughter had talent and her appearances at the Pennyfoot would lead Marion to a star-studded future.

Phoebe was of the opinion that Marion's attempts at show business were only likely to lead the girl into a dark den of iniquity. At the moment, however, she was leading the rest of her troupe on stage, and so far everything seemed to be working out rather well.

Deciding that she had done all she could from the wings, Phoebe hurried back to the ballroom, where she could stand directly in front of the stage. Since the dancers would be looking straight ahead at the audience, this was the best place for them to see her.

Phoebe was firmly convinced that her girls needed to be constantly aware of her vigilant presence in order to complete a successful performance. Without her, the presentation would be doomed to fail.

The fact that the dancers had yet to achieve even a vestige of success did not sway Phoebe from this conviction. She put the blame for their failures firmly on a string of misfortunes caused by ill luck, rather than a lack of discipline and effort.

When she emerged into the ballroom, breathless and flushed with importance, she was delighted to see Cecily seated near the front of the stage. She was rather surprised to see Colonel Fortescue seated next to her.

In order to be rid of the colonel earlier, Phoebe had been forced to agree to join him for a cocktail after the presentation. She was beginning to regret that now, especially if the charming brigadier happened to be attending the ball. It would be very pleasant to spend some time in that man's company. Why, he might even ask her to dance. Phoebe's heart fluttered at the thought.

Turning her attention back to the dance troupe, Phoebe peered anxiously up at the stage. The girls moved slowly toward the center, while the orchestra played some rather pleasant music.

The stage looked magnificent, with a backdrop depicting

the sea behind tall pillars draped in silk greenery, borrowed from the Wellercombe Dramatic Society. It was very tasteful, Phoebe decided.

The music swelled as the musicians sawed furiously on their violins and the harpist plucked even louder at his strings. One by one the bigger girls knelt in position, while the lighter members climbed gingerly onto their shoulders.

The effect was slightly spoiled by Dora's red-rimmed eyes and flushed face, while Marion's laurel wreath had slipped over one eye, causing her to blink repeatedly. Otherwise the tableau was taking shape very nicely, Phoebe decided.

The final position called for the girls on the bottom row to stand, bearing their rather shaky burdens aloft, thus allowing them to position their arms into a classic Greek portrayal. There they would hold the pose throughout the rest of the piece. They would then descend to more comfortable positions where they would remain motionless for the next hour, providing a live backdrop while the guests took to the dance floor.

The girls were not fond of the tableau, complaining bitterly of their aching arms and legs. They would far rather be prancing around the stage but, as Phoebe had reminded them, the tableau provided the opportunity to be on stage and in front of the audience a good deal longer.

The music swelled again, with the pianist pounding the keys in a vain effort to sound like a drum roll. Phoebe held her breath as Marion and her cohorts wobbled upright. The girls on their shoulders clutched each other on the way up, and Phoebe shook her head at them, her fierce frown reminding them they were supposed to be holding a pose.

Finally the maneuver was complete. Less than a minute to go, and the most hazardous part of the presentation would be over. Phoebe let out her breath.

She was about to turn around and send Cecily a smile of triumph when she saw Dora's eyes widen. Phoebe barely had time to anticipate trouble before the wretched girl's mouth opened, and she let out a blood-curdling scream that echoed to the rafters.

The hand that was supposed to be holding a graceful pose stretched out instead, with one finger pointing toward the rear of the ballroom. More screams erupted as the rest of the troupe joined in, then the noise rose to deafening, hysterical shrieks as the entire ensemble collapsed in an inelegant, writhing heap on the stage.

The musicians trailed off one by one, except for the pianist, who seemed oblivious of the commotion and was pummelling the keys with blissful determination.

Furious, Phoebe tugged at the foot of the nearest dancer. "What in the world is the matter with you, Marion? Didn't I tell you to stand firm? Just what do you think you are doing? Get up, all of you, get up!"

The girls paid her no heed. They were all staring over her head at the audience, with varying looks of disbelief and horror on their faces. Sensing that something traumatic could be happening behind her, Phoebe slowly turned.

The first thing she noticed was that the members of the audience were not watching the stage with resigned amusement, which was usually the case when one of her presentations failed so dismally. They were, in fact, without exception, staring toward the back of the ballroom.

Gasps of horror and shrieks of fear rose from the frozen guests. Phoebe followed their gaze, which seemed to be directed toward the balcony. At first she thought it was a graceful figurine hanging there, similar to the laughing cherubs that adorned the alcoves above the balconies.

Upon peering more intently, however, Phoebe noticed that the head of the figurine was at an odd angle. It was then she realized that she and every other occupant of the ballroom were staring at a nude body of a woman. It hung from the neck by a thick, black rope, with long, dark hair mercifully hiding the lifeless face.

Phoebe promptly fainted.

•   •   •

Baxter was on his feet before Cecily fully realized what was happening. Ever since he had sat down at the table and told her Pansy was missing, he had been expecting this moment; she knew that now.

She ignored his command that she stay at the table and followed him through the door, waiting just long enough to lock it behind them. The only other entrance to the balconies lay at the other end of the ballroom. If they were quick enough, they would get there before anyone else and lock those doors as well.

When she reached the first balcony, she looked down. A few people hurried out of the ballroom, some of them undoubtedly morbid enough to want a closer inspection of the corpse.

Ahead of her, Baxter had reached the front balcony, from where the body hung. All the way up the stairs her head had pounded with one question. It had been impossible to see the face of the victim from the dance floor, but the dark hair . . . She tried not to think the worst, but Madeline's words haunted her. *This is the last time I shall be decorating the ballroom. . . .*

No, not Madeline. It couldn't be Madeline. Yet she hadn't seen her friend in the ballroom, although Madeline had assured her she would attend.

Cecily slowed her steps as she made her way toward Baxter.

He was leaning over the balcony, but he straightened just as she reached him. Her heart pounded so heavily she could scarcely breathe, and her lips felt dry and cold when she forced the question through them. "Who is it?"

He spoke sharply, making her jump. "Stay there, Cecily. There is nothing we can do to help her now."

She looked helplessly at him. "Please tell me it isn't Madeline."

He looked puzzled. "Madeline? No, it's the new maid. Pansy."

Cecily closed her eyes, ashamed of her intense relief. Yet

another young girl had just lost her life. This was almost certainly the end of the Pennyfoot. Yet all she could feel right now was a deep thankfulness that the body hanging there was not Madeline's.

"Cecily?" Baxter's concerned voice pulled her together.

"I'm all right, Bax. Poor Pansy. I suppose we should leave her there until the constable gets up here. He must know about this by now." She looked helplessly at him. "Why would anyone do this? Why leave that poor girl hanging in full view of everyone like that?"

"Someone who is extremely disturbed," Baxter said with a look of rage on his face. "A madman, hoping to cause a sensation, no doubt."

Cecily shook her head. "It doesn't make sense. One hidden in a bathtub, one hidden in the cellars, now . . . this."

Baxter ran his hand over his hair, a habit that revealed his agitation. "Mrs. Chubb was worried about her. I looked everywhere for her. I never dreamed she was hanging there."

"You know what this means, of course," Cecily said quietly.

"Yes. It means our murderer is still in the hotel."

"He's a very neat murderer." She pointed to the pile of clothes on the floor, carefully folded with one shoe sitting on top of them. "I would just like to know why he takes one shoe with him."

"As a memento, no doubt," Baxter said grimly.

"We have to close down the hotel," Cecily said, still staring at the forlorn shoe sitting without its partner on the pitiful pile of clothes. "I want to do it before Cranshaw gets the satisfaction of doing it for us."

She'd shocked him. She could see it in his eyes.

"Are you sure? Shouldn't that be a last resort?" he asked.

"It is a last resort. My concern now is for the rest of the staff. As well as the guests, of course."

"Yes, I understand, but surely there is still hope?" His intense gaze rested on her face. "You are not doing this merely to avoid having to follow Cranshaw's orders?''

"I don't think so. I feel this is the right thing to do."

"It isn't like you, Cecily, to give up the battle without a fight."

She was perilously close to tears. Just when she needed his support the most, he was questioning her judgement. "You yourself expressly forbade me to interfere."

"To interfere and put yourself in danger, yes. But I did not expect you to capitulate."

Unable to meet his gaze any longer, she looked down at her hands. "I feel this is something we must do."

After a lengthy pause he said heavily, "Very well. If you are certain."

"Quite certain." She drew a trembling breath. "We shall have to warn everyone. Doors locked, don't go anywhere alone, the usual thing . . ." Her voice broke, and she clenched her hands.

"My dear—" Baxter made a movement toward her, but a heavy pounding on the door made him pause. "Northcott," he said, looking tight-lipped. "I wondered what was keeping him."

Cecily watched him stride to the door and pull it open. She ached for the missed moment when she could have leaned on him for just a little while.

The constable stepped inside, followed closely on his heels by Dr. Prestwick.

Surprised to see him there, Cecily realized he must have attended the ball. He certainly looked very dapper in his black suit and bowtie. She wondered why she hadn't noticed him in the ballroom.

"Where is she?" Northcott demanded, hurrying toward them.

"Still hanging from the railings," Baxter said, sounding just a little caustic. "I assumed you would want to examine the body before we removed it."

"Quite, yes, very good." Northcott peered over the railing. "Looks like it's the same bloke. Strangled with her own stocking.'' He straightened and looked down at the clothes. ''One shoe missing again, I see.''

Prestwick reached them and touched Cecily's arm. ''You are all right?' he asked quietly.

She nodded, touched by his concern. ''Yes, thank you, Kevin. Though I'm devastated, of course. Three of my maids, in the space of two days. This is quite frightening.''

''I agree.'' He looked from Baxter to Northcott. ''We might as well bring the body over and take a look.''

''Right,'' Northcott said, while Baxter merely nodded.

''Cecily, Madeline is waiting for you outside,'' Prestwick said, ignoring her start of surprise at his use of her friend's Christian name.

''I think that's a good idea, Cecily.'' Baxter's waspish tone warned her not to argue with him.

''I will leave you gentleman to your task, then,'' she said, having no real desire to view yet another lifeless body of a young, vibrant girl brought to her death within the walls of the Pennyfoot. ''I will go back to the ballroom and make a formal announcement.''

She received a resigned nod from Baxter and left him to the grisly task. Perhaps he was right, she thought as she headed for the door. Perhaps the Pennyfoot Hotel was cursed. It certainly seemed that disaster was a frequent visitor, beginning with the death of her own husband and followed by so many tragedies.

The noisy chatter out in the hallway ceased as she stepped out from the balcony. Several people stood there, all looking expectantly at her, but it was to Madeline that she spoke, grasping her friend's hand for support. ''It was Pansy,'' she said simply.

Madeline nodded. ''I know. And you thought it was me.''

For a ridiculous moment Cecily was afraid she was going to cry, then she pulled herself together and faced the little group watching her. ''If you would please help me gather everyone back inside the ballroom, I'd like to speak to you all.''

Edward Sandringham stepped out from behind the group. She hadn't seen him standing back in the shadows. "I'll be happy to round up everyone, Mrs. Sinclair, if the rest of you would care to return to the ballroom? I think there'd be less confusion that way."

In spite of her mistrust of the suave gentleman, Cecily felt grateful for his offer. "Thank you, Mr. Sandringham. That would be most kind. Would everyone else please go back to your tables? I'll be there in just a moment or two."

The three couples left without a word, with Sandringham right behind them. Madeline gave Cecily a swift hug. "I'm sorry, Cecily. This is a terrible time for you."

"For all of us. I ache for the families of those poor girls. I must inform Pansy's parents as soon as I have made my announcement."

Madeline looked anxious as she accompanied Cecily back to the ballroom. "You are going to close down the hotel?"

Cecily blinked hard. "It's the last thing in the world I want to do, but I don't see any other choice. It is too dangerous to keep it open with a madman on the loose, and in any case, Inspector Cranshaw will no doubt close it down tomorrow, so I might as well forestall him."

"I can't say I blame you."

Cecily looked at her friend. "Madeline, do you think the Pennyfoot could be cursed?"

Madeline didn't answer at first, but after a moment or two she said quietly, "No, I don't think so. Granted, you have had more than your fair share of tragedy in this hotel, but I prefer to think of it as a run of extremely bad luck."

"The worst," Cecily agreed. "When is it ever going to end?"

Madeline was silent for so long this time that Cecily became alarmed. "What is it?" she demanded. "You are not going to tell me worse is yet to happen, I hope?"

Madeline came to a full stop in the dimly lit hallway and grasped both of Cecily's hands. "Quite the opposite," she said softly. "It is always at the darkest point of the storm that one sees a break in the clouds."

"Well, this is certainly a dark storm." Cecily pressed her lips together for a moment. "Despite all the trouble we've had over the years, we've managed to keep the Pennyfoot open. Even when James died. Now that I am faced with the closure of the hotel, I have to think that this is the end of the Pennyfoot."

"Or a new beginning." Madeline gave her hands a little shake. "Don't give up now, Cecily. You've been so strong."

Cecily lifted her chin, unable to stop a tear escaping. "The worst of it, Madeline, is my promise to James. His last words to me were that I should keep the hotel in the family. If I lose the Pennyfoot now, I will have failed him. I cannot bear the thought of that."

"I am sure James would understand if he knew."

"Perhaps he would," Cecily said evenly, "but in my heart I would always know that I denied a man I loved his dying wish."

"Through no fault of your own. Cecily, listen to me." Madeline let go of her hands and grasped her shoulders. "Take your strength from those who love you, Cecily. The dark days will pass, I promise you. The break in the clouds is very near."

Grateful for her friend's efforts to cheer her, Cecily managed a smile. "Thank you, Madeline. I certainly hope you are right. Now, I had better get to the ballroom and make my announcement."

So saying, she threw off her melancholy and, with a determined thrust of her chin, walked purposefully toward the ballroom.

CHAPTER

❀ 16 ❀

Gertie did her best not to think about what was going on up in the balcony. She'd seen the constable and Mr. Baxter haul the body over the railings and out of view, but she couldn't rid herself of the image of Pansy's naked body hanging limp and lifeless like that.

She hadn't known it was Pansy then, of course. She didn't know that until Samuel came and told her. Now all the staff had been called to the ballroom to hear an announcement from Madam.

Gertie didn't know what it was about; she only knew she was bleeding terrified. For herself, for everyone else, and especially for her babies. She felt alone and helpless, afraid to run and afraid to stay where she was.

Daisy was locked in her room with the children. Just as soon as the announcement was over and she'd cleared the rest of the tables, Gertie intended to make straight for that room and lock the door behind her. She was going sit up all bloody night watching over her babies.

She stacked more plates onto the trolley, then walked around the tables, picking up the condiment sets and cream-ers. No one had been served coffee or tea yet, but none of the guests seemed worried about that.

Most of them stood around in little groups, whispering together, or sat at their tables with a worried look on their faces. Gertie saw Samuel talking to Michel across the room, but she couldn't see Mr. Baxter or Madam. They must still be with the constable, she decided.

She felt sick at the thought of having to look at that body close up. She couldn't think of that thing as being Pansy. Pansy was such a pretty young child, always laughing and joking, though she was scared all right when she had to take them towels up to the bathroom. It was as if she'd known what was going to happen to her.

Gertie shuddered. She kept her eyes down as she plucked the condiment set off a table where a man and his wife sat talking. She didn't want to talk to anyone. Not yet. Not until she was sure she could speak without bawling her eyes out.

She turned to go back to the trolley and came face-to-face with Ross. She hadn't realized he'd come into the room. He stood in front of her, and the anguish in his eyes melted her heart.

"By God, lass, ye're all right."

"'Course I am." She'd tried to sound indifferent, but her voice had wobbled, and she brushed past him, embarrassed by her weakness.

He caught her arm, almost making her drop the silver salt and pepper shakers. "Gertie . . . lass . . . I thought . . . I heard . . ."

She noticed the lump in his throat was moving up and down. Light from the dozens of gaslamps in the crystal chan-delier shone down on his face, and she could almost swear she saw a tear in the corner of his eye.

Aware that anyone in the room could look over and see

them together, she pulled her arm free. "You heard what?" she said, sounding almost rude in her effort to hide her emotion.

"I heard that another maid had been strangled. I went to the kitchen, but no one was there, and I couldn't see you when I first came in."

Suddenly she realized what he was saying. "You thought it were me up there? Strewth, Ross, I'm too blinking heavy for someone to sling me over the balcony like that. He'd bleeding go with me, he would."

For a terrible moment she thought he was going to cry, but then he threw his head back and let out a guffaw that echoed around the room. Oblivious of people watching them, he reached for her and pulled her behind one of the wide pillars supporting the ceiling. There he folded his big arms around her, hugging her so close she couldn't breathe. Or maybe it was the feel of his big body against her cheek that took her breath away.

"Gertie, lass, you'll be the death of me, that you will. For pity's sake, marry me, before I go right out of my head wi' worrying about you and the wee bairns."

"All right," she mumbled, her mouth buried in the rough tweed of his jacket.

His hands jerked her away from him, and his face wore a look of sheer disbelief. "You will? You mean it, lass? Dinna mess with me, Gertie. Tell me the truth."

"I said I bleeding will, didn't I? Now, will you let go of me, you big twit? Everybody's bloody staring at us."

"I dinna care if the whole world is watching us." He grinned at her. "I want to kiss you until you're out of breath."

"Not bloody here, you don't!" She peered around the pillar, mortified to see Madam standing on the stage looking down at everyone. She hadn't noticed her come in, what with all the excitement.

"Later then," Ross whispered in her ear. "After you've

put those shakers down. I don't want them sticking in my chest.''

"Bleeding romantic, aren't we," Gertie said, tossing her head. But she smiled as she said it. The most gorgeous feeling was spreading all over her body, and she was just beginning to enjoy it. She was going to marry Ross. Her babies would have a father, and she'd have a man to take care of and who would take care of her. Just wait until she wrote and told Ethel.

Standing in the middle of the stage, Cecily looked around the now crowded ballroom. The members of her staff stood respectfully against the walls, while the hotel guests took their seats at the tables surrounding the dance floor.

She raised her gaze to the balcony, thankful to see that Pansy's body was no longer hanging there. She felt a sudden longing to have Baxter by her side. Announcing the closure of the Pennyfoot was one of the hardest tasks she had ever been forced to do. She could only hope and pray that she could manage it without breaking down.

She held up her hand, and the chatter died away. The musicians behind her had kept their seats and were waiting silently for her to speak.

Close to the front of the stage, Colonel Fortescue sat with Phoebe, while the dancers seemed to have disappeared. No doubt sent home by their ever-protective dance mistress.

Cecily cleared her throat and in a strong voice began her speech. "My lords, ladies and gentleman. In view of the recent events at this hotel, of which I am sure you are all aware, Inspector Cranshaw of the Wellercombe constabulary has requested that all guests remain at the Pennyfoot until he has questioned everyone on the premises. He will arrive early tomorrow morning and talk to each one of you, after which the guests will be free to leave, should you wish."

She waited for the murmurs rippling through the audience to die down before continuing. "In view of the serious nature of these events, Mr. Baxter and I wish to warn everyone to be on guard and to take extreme precautions for their own safety. We suggest that you stay in your rooms tonight with the doors locked and please, do not venture out alone.''

Amid more murmuring, she paused, bracing herself for the final statement. Unsure if she could utter the words, she started to speak and faltered. Just then she caught a movement out of the corner of her eye and glanced toward the wings. Baxter stood there, watching her with a grave expression on his face.

She stared at him for a long moment. What was it Madeline had said? *Take your strength from those who love you.* Dear Baxter, he did love her. She loved him, also. How she loved him. She loved the Pennyfoot and every member of her staff. And once, she had loved James.

She could not fail her late husband without failing herself. She could not fail her staff, who depended on her. She could not fail Baxter, who believed in her.

She gave him a slight smile, then turned back to the audience. ''Baxter and I deeply regret the inconvenience of these extreme measures, and I can only add that we fervently hope they will not be necessary for much longer. Thank you all for your understanding and for your cooperation. Now, I'm sure the musicians will be happy to play for you so that we can continue with the ball.''

She looked at the conductor, who gave her an answering bow and made his way to the podium. The hum of conversation once more filled the ballroom.

Cecily saw Gertie push her loaded trolley out through the doors, followed closely by Ross. At the back of the room, Kevin Prestwick stood talking to Madeline, while Colonel Chatsworth leaned against one of the stone pillars, watching them both with a strange, brooding look on his face.

She would never have a better chance to talk to everyone, Cecily thought as she hurried over to Baxter.

''You didn't announce it,'' he said when she reached him.

Understanding what he meant, she shook her head. ''You were right, Bax. There's still time. The Pennyfoot will remain open until we are forced to close. Meanwhile, I'm going to ask a few questions if you want to come along.''

''My dear madam, I have no intention of letting you out of my sight until this matter is resolved. At least, that is, unless you are safely locked up in your suite.''

She smiled up at him. ''I was rather hoping you'd say that.''

He followed her down to where Samuel was busily replacing the tablecloths with clean ones.

''I understand that Mrs. Chubb sent you to look for Pansy,'' Cecily said after he'd followed her to a quiet corner.

''Yes, mum. Mrs. Chubb said to fetch her, only I never saw her.''

''What time was that?''

Samuel frowned. ''I think it were about half past ten.''

Just about the time the tableau began, Cecily thought. ''How long had she been gone?''

''Half an hour, Mrs. Chubb said.'' Sam looked apprehensive. ''You think he were waiting for her in the hallway? I warned her to watch out for him.''

''For whom, Samuel?''

''The mad prophet. That's who done it, weren't it?''

Cecily sighed. ''We don't know that yet, Samuel, though I'm sure Inspector Cranshaw will take that possibility into consideration. Did you pass anyone else on your way up there?''

Samuel thought for a moment or two. ''Yes, I did. I saw someone at the other end of a hallway. It were dark at that end, and it was hard to see, but I think it were Colonel Fortescue.''

Cecily frowned. ''That's impossible. The colonel was with me in the ballroom until the start of the tableau. Which hallway was it?''

Samuel creased in brow in thought, then gave a startled look. ''First floor, same as the balconies.''

She exchanged a meaningful glance with Baxter, remembering his comment about the colonel's twin. ''Samuel, you see that gentleman over there?'' She indicated the pillar where the brigadier still lounged.

Samuel looked, and looked again. ''Strewth! Looks just like him, don't he.''

''Indeed he does. Could that be the person you saw?''

''I dunno.'' Samuel still stared at the brigadier in amazement. ''It could have been, I suppose.''

''Thank you, Samuel. I'd appreciate it if you would make sure to accompany to her destination any woman you see walking alone, until we have this cleared up.''

''Yes, mum. I'll do that.''

Leaving him to finish his task, Cecily headed with Baxter across the room to where Chatsworth, apparently bored with the lack of entertainment, was walking toward the doors.

''Brigadier,'' Cecily called out, ''I wonder if I might have a word with you.''

Chatsworth turned with a smile, which faded just a little when he caught sight of Baxter at her side. ''Mrs. Sinclair? Always a pleasure to talk with such an intelligent lady. Quite a speech, what?''

''I wish it hadn't been necessary.'' Cecily glanced over to where Madeline was smiling up at Dr. Prestwick. The doctor gazed down at her as if he'd just discovered gold.

''Quite, quite. This prophet fellow must be terribly sick in the mind, what?''

Cecily returned her attention to Chatsworth. ''Prophet?''

''Yes, the chappie who's running around telling everyone the blasted world is coming to an end.''

''You've seen him?'' Baxter asked sharply.

The brigadier gave him a condescending look. ''My dear chap, I should think everyone in the hotel has seen him. He's everywhere. In the hallways, in the grounds . . . everywhere I turn I see him.''

''I can't understand why I haven't seen him,'' Baxter muttered, his brows drawn together in frustration. ''I've searched all over this hotel.''

"He's wily, all right. Knows whom to avoid, I shouldn't wonder."

Deciding it was time to intervene, Cecily said brightly, "Tell me, Brigadier, at what time did you arrive at the ball?"

The brigadier's bushy white eyebrows jerked upward. "Time? I really couldn't say, madam. Is it important?"

"It's just that Samuel, my stable manager, thought he saw Colonel Fortescue in your hallway about half past ten. But the colonel was with me, so I assume it must have been you, since you look so alike."

"I look like the colonel?" The brigadier sounded genuinely astonished. "Great heavens, madam, you insult me."

"Mrs. Sinclair was merely stating a fact, Brigadier," Baxter said gruffly. "Surely you must have noticed the resemblance?"

Chatsworth appeared to ponder on the suggestion. "Well, now that you come to mention it, I suppose there might be some similarities. White hair and all that, what?"

"Precisely." Baxter looked at Cecily.

"Thank you, Baxter," she murmured, giving him a grateful look. "Brigadier, I don't suppose you saw anyone go into the balcony area while you were in the hallway?"

Chatsworth's eyes gleamed at her beneath the bushy brows as his hand wandered to his tie. In that instant, Cecily had the oddest feeling that she was re-enacting a moment that had already happened before.

"As a matter of fact, madam, I wasn't in the hallway at that time. Since balls and tableaux are not my cup of tea, so to speak, I was in the room next to mine, talking to Mr. Evans, who had also decided not to attend the festivities. We happened to be discussing the possible purchase of a new motorcar."

"I see," Cecily said slowly. Something hovered just at the edge of her mind, but she couldn't quite grasp it.

"I was there from about a quarter past nine until almost eleven. By the time we left his room, all the excitement was over. I'm sure Mr. Evans will be happy to vouch for me."

"Undoubtedly. Thank you for your time, Brigadier."

"Not at all, Mrs. Sinclair."

His dry voice irritated her, and she turned rather sharply to leave, without saying goodnight.

Baxter caught up with her as she crossed the floor. "Cecily? What is the matter, for heaven's sake? You left the brigadier standing there with his mouth open."

"There is something about that man that I really don't like," Cecily muttered. "He can't even pronounce my name correctly."

"Nevertheless, he appears to have a cast-iron alibi for the time of the murder, so I suppose we can rule him out." Baxter sighed. "It does seem as if our killer could be that prophet chap."

"Or someone wanting us to believe he is the culprit." Cecily paused, looking across to where the colonel sat talking earnestly to Phoebe. "I think I'll have a word with Fortescue, in any case."

"Is that wise? You know how the colonel tends to rattle on. All those interminable war stories. I wonder if that's what he's telling Mrs. Carter-Holmes right now?"

Cecily smiled. "If he is, she really doesn't seem to mind."

Phoebe, in fact, appeared to be hanging onto every word the colonel said as Cecily approached the table. "Oh, there you are, Cecily," she said when she caught sight of her. "What a dreadful night. Can you imagine that poor girl? I'm sure I'll have horrific nightmares for weeks."

The colonel shot to his feet and pulled out a chair.

"I trust you are fully recovered from the shock?" Cecily inquired, looking anxiously at Phoebe's pale cheeks.

"Oh, quite, my dear. The colonel has been regaling me with some wonderful stories to keep my mind off the horror of it."

Cecily saw Baxter's eyebrows raise.

"Quite right, old bean," Fortescue said, slapping

Phoebe's shoulder hard enough to make her wince. "We're having a jolly good time, what?"

Cecily quite expected the lady to take a swing at him with her parasol, but she did no such thing. Instead she murmured, "A grand time indeed, Colonel."

Doing her best to disguise her surprise, Cecily sat down at the table. Baxter took the chair next to her, his face carved in stone.

"I'm so sorry about the tableau, Phoebe." Cecily gave her friend a sympathetic smile. "After all your hard work."

"Ah, well, for once it didn't really matter. No one was watching when they collapsed on the floor."

"I hope no one was hurt." Cecily felt quite guilty for not inquiring about the dancers earlier.

"Not at all." Phoebe sniffed. "Those girls could fall off Putney Downs and bounce onto their feet."

Cecily turned to Fortescue, who was gazing at Phoebe as if he couldn't bear to look away. "Did you happen to see the girls fall, Colonel?"

"Oh, yes, indeed, old bean. Rushed right over to help old Phoebs to her feet, what? What? Haven't left her side since."

Old Phoebs? Cecily almost choked at the expression on Baxter's face. What intrigued her even more was the fact that Phoebe didn't seem to mind one bit.

The colonel's statement settled one thing, at least. Samuel couldn't have seen him in the hallway, since he was in the ballroom watching the tableau, as she had thought. Perhaps she should talk to Sid Evans after all, she decided, just to confirm Chatsworth's story.

She looked around the ballroom but could see no sign of that gentleman. Of course, he could be in his room, but she distinctly remembered Chatsworth saying that he had left Evans's room with that gentleman.

"Colonel," she said, tapping his arm to force his attention away from Phoebe, "have you by any chance seen Sid Evans in the ballroom tonight?"

The colonel's brow furrowed. "Sid Evans? Never heard of the chap, old girl. Sorry."

"He's the gentleman who sells motorcars," Cecily prompted. "A thin man, about your height, dark brown hair, clean shaven? He came down to buy a showroom for his vehicles. He must have told you about it. He tries to sell a motorcar to everyone with whom he comes in contact."

The colonel looked at her, puzzlement all over his face. "Sorry, old bean. Never talked to anyone like that. I've only chatted with one fellow this weekend. Brigadier Chatsworth. Great chap. Knows a good deal more than I do about the Boer War, I can tell you. Didn't know half the stuff he's been telling me."

"I really must be going," Phoebe said, making a motion to rise. Both men jumped to their feet, but the colonel took hold of Phoebe's chair and pulled it back.

"Tell Samuel to take you home in a trap, Phoebe," Cecily said, getting to her feet. "I don't want you walking the streets alone at night."

"No need for that," Fortescue said, puffing out his chest. "I will be honored to escort the lady home."

Phoebe fluttered her eyelashes. "I should like that very much, Colonel."

Baxter watched them leave with a wry expression on his face. "I cannot imagine what Mrs. Carter-Holmes can find so fascinating about that man."

Cecily smiled. "Companionship."

"Ah." He looked at her. "I was under the impression that she had aspirations in the direction of the brigadier."

"I was, too. Apparently I was mistaken."

"Well, I just hope he remembers where she lives."

She stared after the retreating figure of the colonel. "I agree that the colonel's memory is not what it should be, but I'm really surprised he doesn't remember Sid Evans."

"Perhaps he's never met him, as he says."

"Then why would Mr. Evans complain about the colonel's boring war stories?"

Baxter shrugged. "Fortescue probably forgot, that's all."

"I'm not so sure," Cecily said slowly. "Something keeps nagging at my mind, yet I can't grasp it. I can't help feeling that I know something that I should pay heed to, yet I can't think what it is."

"You are tired, my dear madam. This has been a very upsetting day. I suggest you retire to your suite and try to rest. Tomorrow your mind will have cleared."

She looked up at him, feeling more troubled than she cared to admit. "I certainly hope so, Baxter," she said quietly. "Because something tells me that whatever it is buried in my mind, it could be extremely important."

CHAPTER
❊ 17 ❊

The strains of a lilting waltz filled the room as Cecily crossed the floor with Baxter at her side. "I don't suppose you would care to take a turn around the floor with me," he murmured, bending close to her ear.

Any other time she would have adored the chance to dance with him. Tonight, however, she had neither the energy nor the inclination. "I'm sorry, Bax. The next ball, I promise." If there was to be a next ball, she silently added.

"I didn't think there was any harm in asking, that's all."

She smiled at him, just as Madeline's voice said softly, "It's wonderful to see lovebirds together, is it not?"

Seeing her friend standing so close to the doctor, looking absolutely breathtaking in a simple white gown, Cecily thought the comment could perhaps apply to Madeline and the doctor.

"Undoubtedly." She turned to Dr. Prestwick. "I trust everything has been taken care of?"

Prestwick nodded. "Northcott has sent the body to the morgue. He's on guard at the front door right now, though I suppose should anyone wish to, he could leave by the French doors right here in the ballroom."

"Or the library, for that matter." Cecily sighed. "Though I imagine suspicion would fall heavily upon whoever did that."

"Quite. Which is why P.C. Northcott is wasting his time, as usual," Baxter put in drily.

Prestwick's gaze flickered, but for once he didn't argue.

"Did you manage to discover anything new about our murderer?" Cecily asked hopefully.

She really didn't expect the doctor to answer. She was therefore quite surprised when Prestwick leaned closer.

"We are obviously dealing with a mass murderer, someone deeply disturbed in the mind," he said, lowering his voice. "Usually these people are driven by an impulse, triggered by something significant to the killer. In this particular case, the missing shoes indicate that our man has a shoe fetish."

Madeline gazed speculatively at the doctor's face as he spoke, apparently fascinated by his words. She certainly appeared smitten by Kevin Prestwick, Cecily thought. He apparently returned the attachment. For once his ardent admiration for a woman actually seemed genuine.

"What exactly does that mean?" Baxter demanded, sounding a trifle impatient.

"It means, my dear fellow, that the killer forms a deep attachment for the shoe, for one reason or another . . . and will go so far as to kill for it. The fact that his victims, up until now at least, have been young, innocent girls, I would say that an unfortunate incident in the killer's past, perhaps involving a young girl, is likely to be the trigger for his compulsions. Since I am not a psychiatrist, however, I am guessing at best."

"It certainly sounds feasible." Cecily shook her head. "I still find it hard to believe that we have lost three young girls in the past two days. It doesn't bear thinking about."

"This will make things difficult for the staff," Madeline murmured. "They are short-handed anyway. Mrs. Chubb was complaining to me about the chaos in the kitchen before all this happened."

"Yes, I know." Cecily lifted her hands in despair. "It is so terribly difficult to find help in Badgers End these days. All our young people are either employed on family farms or seeking their fortune in London."

"We shall have to find them from somewhere," Baxter said with a frown.

"I'd ask Daisy to help out in the kitchen," Cecily murmured, "just for the time being, of course. But then who would take care of the babies?"

"I can take care of them."

Everyone looked at Madeline as if she had said something outrageous.

"Truly?" Cecily clasped her hands together. "Madeline, I think that's a wonderful idea."

"You have had no experience with babies," Baxter said, apparently utilizing his interest as the children's godfather.

"Not with my own," Madeline said carelessly. "I've certainly spent a good deal of time with other women's babies." She sent a sideways glance at Prestwick. "After all, I've been treating enough of them with my potions."

Cecily was intrigued to note that Prestwick seemed unmoved by this provocative statement. "Well, I think it's a marvelous idea," she said, grasping Madeline's hands. "The babies will have a warm, caring person to take care of them who also happens to be a knowledgeable nurse."

"And a doctor who will be glad to offer any assistance necessary," Prestwick added. "I'll be happy to drop in from time to time, just to see how things are going."

Madeline's smile was beautiful to see.

"All that remains is to secure Gertie's permission, and

I'm quite sure she will agree. Especially since it means keeping the babies out of harm's way until this madman is found.'' Cecily beamed up at Baxter. "You see? They will be perfectly safe.''

Baxter inclined his head. "If you say so, madam.''

"I will talk to Gertie first thing in the morning,'' Madeline promised. "It is too late an hour tonight.''

Cecily stifled a yawn. "It is indeed, and I really must retire for the night, if you will both excuse me?''

"Of course.'' Madeline looked concerned. "You do look awfully tired. Have you not been sleeping well?''

Afraid that she was about to offer one of her potions, therefore upsetting the doctor, Cecily said hastily, "Perfectly well, thank you, Madeline. It is just that it has been another tediously long day.''

Madeline nodded. "Take hope, dear Cecily. The dawn is breaking.''

"What on earth did she mean by that?'' Baxter demanded as he accompanied her down the hallway to the stairs.

"Oh, you know Madeline.'' Cecily waved her hand in a vague gesture. "She was just trying to lift my spirits.''

"The only thing that is going to lift your spirits, I wager, is the apprehension of this mad killer.''

"Without doubt, that will help.'' She looked up at him. "But there is one more objective I have in mind that will cure all my ills.''

He eyed her with a look of expectancy in his eyes. "And that is?''

"That is hearing you propose to me again on bended knee.''

His wonderful smile warmed her tired heart. "As soon as time permits,'' he promised her.

He left her with a kiss at her door, and she held that precious moment in her mind as she fell asleep.

She was fortunate the next morning to encounter Sid Evans on his way down to breakfast. He seemed disinclined to talk to her, but she waylaid him by deliberately stepping in front of him in the narrow hallway.

"Mr. Evans! I trust you are sleeping better in your new room?"

"I would sleep a good deal better were this mad prophet apprehended," he muttered. "I do not care to be questioned by the local constabulary. In fact, I bitterly resent the suggestion that we are all under suspicion for these filthy murders. Surely it should be perfectly obvious to everyone that the lunatic wandering around the hotel is the culprit? Why hasn't he been arrested?"

"We can't assume the man's guilt without some evidence," Cecily pointed out. "Rest assured, however, that he will be questioned along with everyone else, once we have located his whereabouts."

"Meanwhile, everyone else has to line up like pigs to the slaughterhouse."

"It is unfortunate, I agree, and I apologize most profusely for the inconvenience." Cecily glanced down the corridor, but most of the guests had already been seated for breakfast, and they were alone. "I didn't see you in the ballroom last night, Mr. Evans. I trust you were not ill?"

"No." Sid Evans scowled. "I don't like dancing and I don't like crowds. I went down to the bar for a drink, instead."

"Oh? I was under the impression that you spent a good deal of the evening in the company of Brigadier Chatsworth."

She was watching his face closely, but could detect no hint of reaction when he said smoothly, "For an hour or two, actually. The chap was interested in purchasing a motorcar. We had a very entertaining conversation."

"So he tells me." Cecily still found it hard to believe these two men had anything in common. In fact, she had never seen them together, not that she could recall, in any case.

She watched Sid Evans rub his jaw, as if it irritated him.

Madeline would no doubt have a remedy for his skin problem, she thought, secretly amused by the vision of this vulgar
man's reactions to Madeline's serene administrations. She
wondered what he would make of her habit of never pre-
scribing a potion without an incantation.

"Well, I hope your business was concluded satisfacto-
rily," Cecily said brightly.

Sid Evans blinked. "I beg your pardon?"

"The purchase of the motorcar," she said, wondering
what she'd said to startle him.

"Oh, quite. Well, we shall see."

"Well, I'll let you go in to breakfast," Cecily said, stepping out of his way. "I hope your interview with the inspector is not as upsetting as you anticipate."

He nodded affably enough, but his expression said quite
clearly that he was prepared for the worst.

Cecily watched him walk off, a feeling of frustration
creeping over her. Everyone seemed so convinced that the
murders were the work of the prophet. Even Baxter had gone
in search of him again this morning.

But then Samuel seemed so sure that he had seen the
colonel in the hallway last night. None of the other guests
fit that description, yet both he and Chatsworth had cast-iron
alibis. Unless Sid Evans was lying. That didn't make much
sense, though, taking into account Dr. Prestwick's evaluation
of a man killing on impulse. Why would Sid Evans cover
up for Chatsworth? Nothing made sense.

So why did she feel certain that somewhere in her mind
lay the answer, and that it had nothing to do with the elusive
prophet, but did in fact have something to do with the man
who had just left?

Gertie burst into the kitchen, feeling as if she were floating
right up to the ceiling. It wasn't decent to feel so happy,
what with all the tragedy going on around the hotel, but she
couldn't help it. She was going to burst unless she could tell
someone.

Michel was alone in the kitchen, pushing the heavy pots and pans around on the stove and muttering gibberish to himself. Gertie opened her mouth to tell him the news, then shut it again. Maybe it would be better to wait for Mrs. Chubb, she decided. Michel was likely to fly off the handle at the thought of her leaving.

Gertie walked over to the window and looked out across the kitchen yard. It seemed like she'd lived at the Pennyfoot all her life. She'd miss it all right, especially Mrs. Chubb and Daisy, even Michel. She'd missed Doris since she left, though she was glad Doris had done so well for herself in London.

It must be nice to be on the stage, she thought, grabbing hold of a big iron cauldron. All those people looking up at you, watching you perform. Only that life wasn't for people like Gertie Brown. She didn't have talent, not like Doris. All she had was a deep longing to belong somewhere. Really belong.

That's what had made it so hard to decide to leave the Pennyfoot. She'd felt like she belonged there. It was home to her. Her only home.

Now she was going all the way to Scotland to a new home. A new land. Strange people she'd never met and probably wouldn't understand at first. Sometimes it was hard to even understand her Ross when he talked fast.

Her Ross. Her uneasiness vanished when she thought about him. He was strong, her Ross. He'd look after her and the babies, wouldn't he. He'd even promised to bring her back for a holiday at the Pennyfoot.

Gertie grinned happily. Wouldn't that be something? Her and the babies staying at the Pennyfoot Hotel instead of working in it? She wouldn't half enjoy that, she would.

"I don't know what in the world you can find to smile about, Gertie Brown, but if you stand there much longer with that pot in your hand, I'll give you the sack."

Gertie's dream world vanished at the sound of Mrs.

Chubb's voice. "You can't give me the bleeding sack, Mrs. Chubb."

The housekeeper bristled, glaring at Gertie with her arms crossed over her bosom. "Why not, might I ask?"

Gertie put the cauldron down and skipped over to her. "Because I'm giving me bloody notice, that's why. I'm going to marry Ross McBride. He gave me a ring and everything."

Mrs. Chubb's face turned red. "I'm so happy for you, duck, though I didn't think you would do it this soon. Never mind, we'll manage somehow . . ."

Her voice trailed off, and Gertie sobered at once. "Bleeding heck, I forgot about that. If I leave, you won't have no one except Daisy."

"And she's going to London." The housekeeper fanned her flushed face with her apron. "I don't know what I'm going to do. That I don't."

Before Gertie could answer, the door opened, and Madeline swept in, her filmy blue gown floating behind her. "There you are, Gertie. I was hoping I'd find you here. Mrs. Sinclair needs Daisy to help out in the kitchen, so I'm offering to take the babies back to my house until things get back to normal here. If they ever do."

Gertie stared at her. "You want to take my babies to your house?"

"If that's agreeable to you, of course. Daisy won't be able to look after them, and I'd love to have them."

Gertie looked at Mrs. Chubb for help. She wasn't at all sure how she felt about that. She liked Miss Pengrath and everything, but there were those what said she was a bloody witch, and she didn't want to leave her babies with someone what could turn them into bleeding frogs or something.

Madeline must have seen the doubt on her face, as she said quietly, "I'll understand if you'd rather not, Gertie. All I can say is that I'd give them the very best of loving care, and Dr. Prestwick has promised to look in several times a day, just to make sure all is well."

"Dr. Prestwick?" Gertie repeated, still looking at Mrs. Chubb.

The housekeeper gave her a smile of encouragement. "I think it's an excellent idea, Gertie. The twins will love Madeline and they will be safer away from the hotel until that madman is caught."

"Well, that's true," Gertie muttered.

Across the room, Michel crashed a pot down on the cast-iron stove. "Will you please make up your mind! I am waiting for ze eggs for ze omelettes, *s'il vous plait.* Or do I have to go out to the chicken house myself this morning?"

Gertie jumped. "All right, Miss Pengrath. I'll come with you and get them ready."

"Send Daisy back here, then," Mrs. Chubb said, giving her a nod of approval. "And get back as soon as you can."

"All right, I'm hurrying as fast as I can bleeding go." What was important right now was to get her babies' things packed up and then say goodbye to them for a while.

It would hurt like bleeding hell to let them go, but at least she'd have peace of mind until the crazy prophet were caught. Then she could tell everyone her news.

She followed Madeline out of the door, feeling some of her happiness slip away. Mrs. Chubb was going to take it hard, she knew. She felt like she was deserting the hotel just when it needed her the most. Maybe she could persuade Ross to stay a while longer, until they got the staff problems sorted out.

Strewth, she thought as she stomped down the hallway to her room. Why was it that nothing was ever flipping perfect? Why was it so bloody hard to please everyone? Why did so many people have to get bleeding hurt when all she was trying to do was find a little happiness for herself and her twins?

Because that was life, that's what, she answered herself. No matter how hard, or frustrating, or disappointing it was, that was life. She'd rather have it that way than watch the whole bleeding world come to an end.

Without warning, her thoughts scattered and flew as she turned the corner and walked straight into Madeline, who had stopped dead for some strange reason. Looking over the other woman's head, Gertie caught her breath.

A man stood barring the way in the narrow corridor, his hands outstretched toward them. His eyes gleamed strangely above a tangled beard, and he was whispering something she couldn't catch.

"Who are you?" Madeline demanded, her voice tight with shock. "What do you want?"

"I know who he is," Gertie whispered through lips that felt cold and stiff. "That's the bleeding mad prophet. Hang onto your bloody shoes, for Gawd's sake."

CHAPTER

❧ 18 ❧

Cecily crossed the foyer to where P.C. Northcott sat, looking bleary-eyed from his sleepless night. "Are they sending someone to relieve you?" she asked as the constable barely suppressed a yawn.

"The h'inspector 'imself will be arriving shortly," Northcott announced. "I shall leave everything in his capable hands just as soon as he gets here. Though I can tell you, Mrs. Sinclair, he won't be happy to hear about all these murders."

"I don't suppose he will," Cecily murmured. "I understand you saw no sign of our prophet last night?"

"No, m'm, I didn't. Not a sign of him."

"Well, thank you, Constable. I suppose I should be—" She cut off as an eerie scream echoed up the steps from the kitchen.

"Strewth! What was that?" Northcott rose to his feet, his startled gaze on Cecily's face.

"I have no idea, but I think we should find out." Without waiting to see if he followed her, Cecily hurried to the steps and ran down them.

The scene that met her eyes stopped her heart. Gertie stood flattened against the wall, her hand over her mouth. Her gaze was on Madeline, who stood with her back to the steps, her hands held out in front of her, fingers pointed at the cowering figure of a bearded man.

As Northcott stumbled down the stairs behind her, the man opened his mouth and emitted another shrill scream that chilled Cecily's bones.

"Bloody hell," Gertie wailed, edging toward Cecily.

The prophet stared with wild eyes at the constable charging toward him. "Get her away from me!" he screamed. "She's a witch! Get her away from me!"

"Stay where you are!" Madeline's voice rang out, and Cecily wasn't sure if she was addressing the shivering man or the constable, who had come to a dead stop just a foot or two away from Madeline's erect figure.

"I won't harm you," Madeline said softly. "I just want to help you."

The man began to cry in a high-pitched voice that sounded eerily like a child's keening. "You can't help me. No one can help me. The world is coming to an end, and no one can stop it."

"Yes, I can." Madeline actually appeared to grow taller. "I have the power to do anything. I will not let the world come to an end, I swear it."

Her words stopped the prophet's crying, but he continued to sniff childishly, his wary gaze fixed on Madeline's face.

"Go with the policeman," she said. "He wants to help you, too. He will take care of you." She looked back at P.C. Northcott. "He will go quietly, I'm sure."

Northcott, who looked a little dazed, marched forward and took the man's arm. "Come on, there's a good chap. Let's go down to the station and have a nice talk.''

He led the quivering man past Cecily, touching the brim of his helmet as he did so. ''I'd appreciate it if you'd inform the inspector when he gets here, Mrs. Sinclair. I'm sure you'll have nothing to worry about from now on.''

''Thank you, Constable. I'll be sure the inspector gets the full story.'' She watched the burly policeman half drag his reluctant prisoner up the steps and disappear.

''Bloody hell, how did you do that?'' Gertie demanded, looking at Madeline in awe. ''All you did was point at him, and he bleeding fell to pieces.''

''Mind over matter,'' Madeline said, smiling. ''Why don't you get the babies ready for me, Gertie. I'll be along in a minute. I'd like to have a word with Mrs. Sinclair first.''

''Yes, Miss Pengrath.'' Gertie dropped a hasty curtsey in Cecily's direction, then fled down the hall.

''Are you all right?'' Cecily asked anxiously. ''That must have been quite an ordeal.''

''Not really.'' Madeline brushed her hands together as if dismissing the incident. ''The man is harmless, Cecily. I'd swear to it. Just a little disturbed, that's all. He's not a killer.''

Cecily nodded unhappily. ''After having seen him, I'm inclined to agree, Madeline. If so, our murderer is still at large, though I suppose we shall have to let the police decide on that.''

''I just don't want you to be lulled into a false sense of security.'' Madeline's lovely brown eyes looked troubled as she gazed intently into Cecily's face. ''I sense danger surrounding you, Cecily. Please take extra care that you are not alone anywhere until this man is caught.''

''I will. Don't worry, Madeline. Take those babies home where they will be safe. I will feel a lot easier in my mind.''

Madeline reached out and touched Cecily's shoulder. ''Beware, my friend. There is still a dark cloud before the skies will clear.''

Smothering her uneasiness, Cecily left her friend and

made her way back up the steps to the foyer. The inspector was due to arrive very shortly, and still the identity of the murderer had not been uncovered.

If Madeline was right about the prophet, then one of the guests could very well be the guilty party. Again she tried to grasp the niggling thought at the edge of her mind, but it slipped away once more.

Reaching the foyer, she saw Baxter enter the front door and called out to him. He hurried over to her, his face anxious.

"I heard that Northcott has that crazy prophet in custody," he said, running a hand over his hair. "Was anyone else hurt?"

"No." She thought about telling him of Madeline's conviction that the man was innocent, but knowing how skeptical Baxter was of her friend's strange powers, she thought better of it. "Gertie was a little frightened. She was there when the man confronted Madeline."

"What happened?"

Cecily shrugged. "Madeline handled it in her own proficient way. She had a very calming effect on the man. He was quite docile when the constable led him away."

"Thank the Lord for that. I suppose we can all relax now. Cranshaw won't have to question everyone, and you won't have to close down the Pennyfoot."

"I imagine the inspector will still want to ask a few questions."

"Where is Miss Pengrath now?" Baxter looked around, as if expecting her to be in the foyer. "Has she taken the babies home with her yet?"

"No, she hasn't. She's with Gertie, packing up a few things. As a matter of fact, I wanted to talk to you about that. She'll need some help getting them home, and I was wondering if you would mind taking her home in one of the traps. I'd send Samuel, but they are so short-handed in the kitchen . . ."

"Of course I'll take her." He smiled down at her. "I'm

sure you can handle the inspector until I get back.''

''I'll do my best.'' She watched him stride toward the kitchen steps, wishing she could throw off her uneasiness that easily.

What she needed, she decided, was a breath of fresh air to clear the cobwebs from her mind. A few minutes in the roof garden would work wonders, as it had always done in times of stress. Baxter would have taken the key with him, she thought, but there was a set of master keys in his office.

She found them in a desk drawer and hurried back to the foyer. Eagerly she climbed the stairs, anxious now to feel the quiet, calming effect of gazing at the ocean and the picturesque bay. There was something about watching a lone seagull in flight that always soothed her nerves.

She reached the first landing and was about to turn into the next flight of stairs when a movement in the shadows made her jump. Her heart skipped crazily for an instant, and her hand went to her throat as she stared up at the tall, silent figure in front of her. ''Mr. Sandringham! You quite startled me.''

''My apologies, Mrs. Sinclair. I was wondering if you knew when the inspector is due to arrive. I understand he will be questioning us all about the unfortunate deaths of those poor children.''

''Yes, he will. It's a necessary part of his investigation, I'm afraid.''

''Quite.'' He paused, looking down at her feet. ''I hope you don't mind me mentioning it, Mrs. Sinclair, but one of your shoelaces is untied. I should hate to see you trip over it and take a nasty fall. Perhaps you would permit me to tie it for you?''

Before she could protest, he dropped to one knee and proceeded to tie up the shoelace with painstaking care. She glanced around, praying that no one would catch sight of him on bended knee in front of her. All she needed was for Baxter to hear of it and form the wrong impression.

She stared down at the top of Edward Sandringham's

head, beginning to feel a little disquieted at the length of time he was taking. A vision popped into her mind of a forlorn pile of clothes with one shoe sitting on top of it.

All of a sudden she felt very cold.

She was alone on the landing, helpless against an attack from this husky man. What good would it do to call out? The guests were all enjoying breakfast in the dining room, which was where Edward Sandringham was supposed to be, now that she thought about it.

Baxter had more than likely left by now with Madeline, and the constable was on his way back to the station with the man he assumed was the killer. The man everyone had assumed was the killer. When, in fact, at this very minute the murderer could be kneeling right in front of her.

Now that she thought about it, she didn't remember seeing Sandringham in the ballroom last night. Yet he had stepped out from behind the little group outside of the balcony doors after Pansy's body had been discovered.

He wasn't actually touching her, just the laces of her shoe. All she had to do was kick him hard in the face and make a mad dash down the stairs. She braced herself, trying desperately to find the nerve. Just one, swift kick—

"There you are!" Edward Sandringham rose and smiled down at her. "I'm sorry it took so long. I have a touch of arthritis in my fingers. Too many years in the tropics, I'm afraid."

Her throat was so tight she could hardly speak. She could feel a pulse in her throat throbbing furiously beneath her high lace collar. "Thank you, Mr. Sandringham. I am much obliged."

His expression changed. "Are you all right? You sound rather hoarse."

"I'm quite well, thank you." She moved a step away from him, still shaken by her panic. "I don't wish to keep you from breakfast."

"Oh, that's all right. I never eat breakfast. I prefer to save my appetite for the midday meal."

"I see." All she wanted to do now was get away from him and escape to the roof. "If you'll excuse me?"

"Mrs. Sinclair, there is something I should like to discuss with you, if you have a minute? It's rather important."

"Perhaps it could wait, Mr. Sandringham? I was on my way up to the roof garden."

"Splendid. Then I'll accompany you." To her utter consternation, he took a firm hold of her arm and started up the stairs, propelling her helplessly along with him.

"He isn't a murderer, you know," Madeline said as the chestnut clopped along the almost deserted esplanade.

Baxter barely heard her. He was too busy contemplating the depressing lack of guests in the town. By now the sands should have been swarming with happy youngsters, watched over by uniformed nannies and fond parents.

The Punch and Judy show, which had opened just the week before, was playing to a dismal group of no more than a dozen spectators, instead of the usual fifty or more.

Even the donkeys, accustomed to trotting along the sands with delighted children on their backs, were still tethered in the shade of the cliffs. As for the souvenir shops lined along the esplanade, only a handful of ladies peered into their bay windows.

Realizing at last that Madeline had spoken, he murmured politely, "I beg your pardon?"

"I said he isn't a murderer."

"Who isn't?"

"That poor little man who thinks the world is coming to an end. He is quite harmless. Just a little disturbed, that is all."

Baxter's mind snapped back to attention. He glanced over his shoulder to where she sat behind him with a struggling twin in each arm. "What did you say?"

Madeline gave him a look of exasperation. "That poor man, whom the constable is no doubt bombarding with asinine questions at this very minute, is not a killer. I'd stake my life on it.''

He half turned to look at her. ''What makes you think so?''

Madeline gave a careless shrug that irritated him. ''I just know. Call it intuition, a good sense of character, whatever you like. I just know.''

Baxter stared at her, the reins slack in his hands. He had never put much stock in Madeline's wild predictions and hoary warnings. There had been just enough conviction in her voice, however, to alert him. One thing he would have to admit, Madeline Pengrath was an uncannily accurate judge of character.

She had impressed him in the past with her observations, and he had an uneasy feeling that she was right this time about the mad prophet. Nevertheless, he felt compelled to say, ''I certainly hope you are mistaken.''

''I wish I were.'' She leaned toward him, her worried expression intensifying his unrest. ''Baxter, please take special care of Cecily.''

At first he wondered if Cecily had told her friend about his intended proposal and that Madeline was referring to Cecily's future in general. But then she said something that greatly disturbed him.

''I'm afraid for her, Baxter. I have a premonition that she is going to need your help quite desperately, and soon.''

He turned his attention back to the road, flicking the reins lightly across the chestnut's back. Madeline and her premonitions—she'd have him acting as crazy as all her other followers if he listened to her.

Yet try as he might, he could not rid himself of the nagging anxiety that her words had aroused. He flicked the reins again, urging the chestnut into a canter, anxious now to be back at the Pennyfoot.

What had he said to Cecily just the night before? *I have no intention of letting you out of my sight until this matter is resolved.* Foolishly he had been so anxious to have the matter resolved he had allowed himself to believe that the arrest of the prophet had solved the problem. He should have known better than to make rash judgements.

It seemed an eternity before he pulled up in front of Madeline's cottage. It took several minutes more to unload the babies and all their belongings, and carry them up the long gravel path to the door.

He waited, inwardly seething with impatience, while Madeline fussed about where she wanted the cots to go, then moved them twice before she was satisfied.

"Please let us know should you have any problem with the babies," he said, dropping a swift kiss on the downy head of each of his godchildren. "We are but minutes away."

"Thank you, but I'm sure I can manage very well." Madeline looked quite radiant as she showed him out. "Dr. Prestwick will be calling on me at intervals."

Baxter raised his eyebrows, wondering just when that particular feud had been settled. He didn't waste any time questioning her, however. All he could think about was getting back to the hotel and finding Cecily safe and sound. Only then could he laugh at his irrational fears.

CHAPTER

❀ 19 ❀

Cecily smiled to herself as she accompanied Edward Sandringham down the stairs from the roof garden. She couldn't wait for Baxter to return so that she could give him the exciting news.

How foolish she had been to suspect Edward of being the killer. If he hadn't knelt to tie up her shoelace, she would never have had such a silly notion. All this business of the missing shoes had twisted her thinking.

She paused as she reached the second floor landing. Shoes. Of course. An idea slowly formed in her mind. An idea so simple she didn't know why she hadn't thought of it before.

The killer had stolen one shoe from each of his victims. If he was a guest in the hotel, then the missing shoes could possibly be hidden in his room. If she could find the shoes, then it would be feasible to assume that she had also found the murderer.

Breakfast was still being served in the dining room. If she hurried she'd have time to search at least a couple of rooms, and the first one on her list was Sid Evans's room at the end of the hallway.

She turned to Sandringham, who was waiting for her to go down the next flight of stairs. "If you will excuse me, Edward, I have a couple of things that need my attention. I will talk to Baxter and let you know our decision by tomorrow noon. Perhaps we can meet in the library?"

"Wonderful. I hope we can come to a satisfactory arrangement."

She smiled at him. "I'm quite sure we shall."

She waited for him to turn the corner, then hurried down the hallway. The master keys were in her pocket. It shouldn't take her long to make a quick search of the room. There might even be time to search the brigadier's room as well.

She reached the door and looked over her shoulder to make sure she was not observed. For one fleeting moment she hesitated, knowing how cross Baxter would be that she hadn't waited for him.

There was no time, she assured herself. The guests would soon be finished with breakfast, and then Inspector Cranshaw would be arriving and she wouldn't have another chance. It had to be now.

She rapped on the door, waited for a heart-pounding minute or two, then slipped the key into the lock and turned it. She opened the door cautiously and peered inside the room. It was empty.

Quickly she slipped inside and closed the door quietly behind her. The wardrobe seemed the logical place to start, she decided. Her feet made no sound on the soft Axminster carpet as she crossed to the wardrobe and opened the door.

Sid Evans, as she had already surmised, was not an orderly person. Clothes hung half off their hangers, and a couple of suit jackets had fallen all the way to the floor.

Cecily picked them up, more from habit than anything. Then she dropped them again, shocked beyond belief. She hadn't really expected to strike gold on the first try. There they were, however, stacked neatly together. Three identical, highly-polished black oxfords. The uniform shoes of the Pennyfoot Hotel.

She straightened, then turned with a gasp as the door to the room opened without warning. For a minute her fear held her immobile, then she let out her breath.

"Brigadier Chatsworth! What a fright you gave me. I'm so glad you're here. I need your help."

"Mrs. Sinclair. I was looking for Mr. Evans, but—"

She saw his gaze move down to the shoes she held. His expression didn't change, but his hand went straight to his tie.

It was then that she knew what it was that had been nagging at her. She stared at Chatsworth, her mind rapidly sifting through the possibilities. "I came in here to listen to the fireplace," she said, trying desperately to sound unconcerned. "Mr. Evans has been complaining about noises in there."

"I see." His gaze remained fixed on the shoes, and she wished now that she'd left them where she'd found them.

"I found these," she said, holding them up for his inspection. "Someone must have left them here."

"Indeed. I do wonder who that could be."

His voice had changed to one that was also familiar to her. As if in a bad dream, she watched in horror as Chatsworth lifted his hand and slowly peeled off his beard and mustache. With his other hand he pulled the white wig from his head. "It's really unfortunate that you should choose this moment to snoop around, Mrs. Sinclair."

There it was, the emphasis on the beginning of her name. Everything clicked into place as she stared into the face of Sid Evans.

Baxter raced along the hallway to the dining room, his feeling of urgency more potent than ever. Several of the guests passed him on their way out, and gave him curious glances when he curtly brushed by them without a word.

One look around the half-deserted room assured him that Cecily was not there. He had already tried her suite, as well as his office, the drawing room, and the library. All that was left now was the kitchen, then the grounds.

Gertie was alone in the kitchen when he flung open the door. She stared at him, a look of horror on her face. "Mr. Baxter! Whatever is it? Not someone else bleeding murdered, is it?"

"I sincerely hope not," Baxter said grimly. "I'm looking for Mrs. Sinclair. Have you seen her recently?"

"Madam? I saw her upstairs a little while ago. Talking to that blinking nosy Mr. Sandringham, she was—"

He didn't wait to hear more. Letting the kitchen door swing to, he bounded up the steps once more to the foyer.

He was just in time to see Edward Sandringham disappear through the front door. He raced after him, shouting his name, and burst out onto the steps, almost colliding with the gentleman who had paused to wait for him.

"Mr. Baxter," Sandringham said in surprise. "Is something wrong?"

"Mrs. Sinclair," Baxter rapped out. "What have you done with her?"

Sandringham shook his head in bewilderment. "I haven't done anything at all with her, my dear fellow. The last time I saw her, just a few minutes ago, she was on her way to attend to some matter or other."

Baxter silently cursed himself for his irrational haste. It was quite obvious the man had no idea why he was so upset. "I beg your pardon, Sandringham. It's just that I'm concerned about Mrs. Sinclair. Where did you last see her?"

"On the second floor. I believe she was on her way to one of the rooms."

"To search it, no doubt." Baxter cursed under his breath. "I should have known." He leapt for the door and rushed through it, followed closely by Sandringham, who apparently had been infected by Baxter's anxiety.

Together they rushed up the stairs, with Baxter taking the lead on the second-floor landing. Looking down the hallway, he felt a jolt of apprehension. The door to Sid Evans's room stood ajar.

He reached it in a few giant strides and peered inside. The room was empty, but lying on the floor in the middle of the carpet were three black oxford shoes. His heart seemed to stop when he saw his master keys lying next to them.

"He's got her!" he shouted at Sandringham. "He wouldn't have taken her down the stairs. Too many people. There's only one place I haven't looked yet . . . the roof garden. I'm going up there. Call Northcott . . . and Dr. Prestwick . . . then get Samuel. He's in the stables."

"Right!" Sandringham leapt to obey, and, satisfied his orders would be carried out, Baxter headed for the steps to the roof garden. Never in his life had he felt such fear. How much time had Evans had? Cecily could well be dead by now.

His mind violently rejected that possibility. He couldn't lose her now, just when they were about to start a new life together. She had to be alive.

His lungs ached, and his legs trembled as he took the steps three at a time. For a moment he panicked when he thought the door to the garden was locked, but something must have been wedged against it, as it gave way when he put his shoulder to it.

He stumbled out, blinking in the brilliant sunlight, and paused to get his bearings. As he did so, he caught sight of a man struggling to lift something over the wall.

He realized with horror that the man was Sid Evans, and the burden he seemed so eager to get rid of was a limp body. He recognized the clothes instantly. The body was Cecily.

Like the sudden onslaught of a winter storm, it seemed as if everything turned cold and black. He felt a rage such as he'd never even imagined before. This man was trying to take away from him the only person in the world who truly mattered to him. He would die before he'd allow that to happen.

With a strength that seemed to well up from deep within him, he lunged forward, hands outstretched. Sid Evans threw one desperate glance over his shoulder and gave his burden an almighty heave.

Cecily's head and shoulders hung over the edge, and she began to slide as Sid Evans grabbed her feet for one final push. With a howl of fury, Baxter reached her and grabbed hold of her long skirt.

With one hand he fought off the frantic man while he hauled Cecily safely back across the wall, where she crumpled in a heap onto the ground.

Sid Evans backed away from the enraged man facing him. He looked over at the door, to which Baxter effectively blocked the way.

"You are going to die for this, you bastard!" Baxter roared. "You'll go to the gallows, and I'll dance on your damn grave!"

He took a step toward Evans, fists raised, intending to beat the man senseless before handing him over to the police.

Instead, Evans spun around and clambered up to the sloping roof.

Afraid he was going to lose him, Baxter clambered up after him. He had taken only two steps when Evans, in a desperate attempt to cross the roof, recklessly balanced on the uppermost ridge. For one breathless second or two, it seemed as if he would make it across, but then, with a bone-chilling howl, he overbalanced and fell headlong to the brick courtyard below.

For a moment Baxter felt sick, until he reminded himself what the man had done, not only to three young girls, but to his beloved Cecily.

He was almost afraid to approach her limp body lying so lifeless and still on the rough ground. My God, if the man had strangled her, he could not live with himself.

His reluctant gaze moved down to her feet, and hope

sprang in his breast when he saw that she wore both of her shoes, as well as her stockings.

He dropped down beside her and cradled her in his arms. His fingers went immediately to her wrist, where he detected a faint but steady pulse. Tears welled in his eyes. She was at least alive.

Her cheek was grazed, and he pulled a handkerchief from his pocket and gently dabbed at the bleeding wound. "Cecily, my dearest love," he whispered. "Come back to me. I need you so much. I could not bear to lose you. I cannot live without you."

He bowed his head, resting his forehead against hers. This was his fault. He should have been by her side, protecting her. Dear God, if only she would recover, he would never leave her side again. He began muttering again, the words tumbling out in a heartfelt plea. "Cecily, my love, forgive me. Give me one more chance, and I swear I will protect you and guard you with my life until the day I die."

"If that is your proposal, then I accept."

At first he thought he was hearing things. He lifted his head and stared down at her. Her eyes were still closed, and her face was deathly pale, but she wore a smile, and it was the most beautiful smile he'd ever seen in his entire life.

A tear fell unashamedly from his cheek and splashed on her nose. "Cecily, lie still. Where do you hurt?"

"My head. He smashed it against the wall."

"The bastard. He got what he deserved."

"Where is he now?"

"Lying in the courtyard."

"Dead?"

"Considering he fell head first from the roof, I should certainly imagine so."

He felt a shiver run through her. "How awful."

"No more so than what he did to those poor young girls . . . and you."

At long last she opened her eyes. "Is it raining?"

"Only tears from my heart."

Her eyes softened. "Oh, Baxter, I'm so sorry I worried you."

He gathered her close and kissed her gently. "Hush, my love. Don't talk. The doctor should be here soon to look at you."

"All I have is a bad headache. I have powders that will cure that."

"You are not moving until the doctor gets here."

She gave him a look that was all too familiar. "Piffle. Just because I promised to marry you doesn't mean I'm going to allow you to issue me orders."

He wrinkled his brow. "I was afraid that might be the case."

"Does that mean you've changed your mind?"

He dashed the back of his hand across his eyes. "Never, dear madam. The only thing that has changed is the date we will be married. The sooner we are wed, the better I shall be able to take care of you."

To his relief she looked almost her old self when she smiled. "In that case, Bax, help me up. I should hate for one of the staff to find us in such a compromising position. Besides, I have something of great importance to discuss with you. Something that will change our entire future together. And I need to be on my feet to do it."

CHAPTER
❀ 20 ❀

It was some time later before Cecily was able to tell Baxter the news that she was bursting to share. Inspector Cranshaw had arrived and insisted on meeting with Cecily in the library, while Baxter assisted the constable and Prestwick with the removal of Sid Evans's body.

By the time order had been restored, the staff reassured, and the guests informed, it was time to serve the midday meal. It wasn't until late in the afternoon that Cecily managed to escape to the roof garden once more to meet with her future husband.

"I still have not proposed to you in the manner I envisioned," Baxter said as they stood side by side at the wall.

Cecily looked across the wide expanse of glittering water, to where the fishing boats bobbed in the harbor. Tiny thatched cottages lined the curve of the bay, and behind them the white walls of the cliffs rose to the green, lush carpet of Putney Downs.

She felt a sudden pang of nostalgia, knowing that what she had in mind would take her away from the quiet beauty of this little seaside town that had been her home for so many eventful years.

"You were on bended knee, were you not?" She turned to smile at him. "And I gave my answer."

"But I did not give you this." He drew a small box from his pocket and handed it to her.

Her hands trembled when she opened it, and her breath caught when sunlight flashed upon the brilliant diamond nestled in a circle of emeralds.

"I trust it is to your liking?"

His voice had revealed his anxiety, and she lifted her face for his kiss. "I adore it, Bax. It is the most beautiful ring I have ever seen."

He took the ring from her and slipped it on her finger. For a long moment he looked at her, then cleared his throat. "Well, now that we have that settled, what is it that you have to tell me that has you bubbling with so much excitement?"

She reluctantly tore her gaze away from the ring sparkling on her finger. "We are to meet with Edward tomorrow at noon."

Baxter wrinkled his brow. "Edward?"

"Sandringham."

"Isn't that just a little familiar? I had no idea you knew him well enough to call him by his Christian name."

She grinned, delighted by his perturbed expression. "There is no need to look so put out, Baxter. Edward Sandringham happens to be a cousin of my late husband."

Baxter's eyebrows shot up. "Sandringham is James's cousin?"

"Yes. I had heard no mention about him from James, but it appears the two of them fell out many years ago. Edward has been out of the country until recently, at which time he learned of James's death and my struggle to maintain the Pennyfoot.''

''But why did he not tell you who he was when he arrived?''

Cecily looked back at the ocean, feeling again that strange bittersweet sensation at the thought of leaving. ''Because he wants to buy the Pennyfoot. He wanted to investigate the property and felt he would get a truer evaluation if no one knew who he was or what he was about.''

Baxter was silent for a long time, while she waited anxiously for his reaction. Finally he murmured, ''Is he aware of the heavy debts involved?''

''Yes, he has gone into things pretty thoroughly. He wants to remodel the hotel and turn it into a modern but very select country club for the motoring crowd. Apparently there is a great call for this type of establishment.''

''I see.''

Again the lengthy pause made her anxious.

''How does this sit with you?'' Baxter asked at last.

She took a deep breath, then turned to look at him. ''Edward is prepared to make a very generous offer. More, I suspect, than what the hotel is actually worth. You have complained recently that the Pennyfoot is taking up too much of our time. I think you are right. We are not young people anymore. I would like to spend more time with my husband and enjoy whatever years we have left. I think we should sell.''

He took her hands in his, hope spreading across his face. ''You are sure?''

''I am sure.'' She smiled. ''After all, my promise to James will be satisfied. The Pennyfoot will remain in the family.''

Apparently caught up by emotion, he raised both her hands to his lips. ''I can't tell you how happy this makes me.''

''You don't have to, Bax. I know this is what you have wanted for some time. The staff will have to be told, of course. Edward has assured me that he will keep anyone who wishes to work for him.''

"You will miss the hotel.''

"Yes, but I'll miss the people more.'' Already she was beginning to sense the ache. "But I feel in my heart that it's time. We shall now have time to visit Michael and Andrew, and I shall be quite busy taking care of my new husband and our home together.''

"How would you like to live in London for a while?''

"I should like that. Anywhere, as long as it is with you.''

He held her close for a moment or two, then put her away from him. "You have yet to tell me what the inspector had to say.''

"Ah, yes.'' Glad of the excuse to change the subject, she looked down once more to admire her ring. "It seems that our Sid Evans was something of a celebrity in London. The police have been searching for some time for the man who has killed at least a dozen or so young women over the past three years. When Inspector Cranshaw mentioned the missing shoe to Scotland Yard, he was told about the Shoe Strangler, as he was known, and immediately suspected that our killer was the same man. He returned early this morning with the intention of warning us and of closing down the hotel.''

"Good Lord.'' Baxter ran his hand over his hair. "To think you were in the hands of that maniac.''

"Well, thanks to you, it all turned out well. Apparently Sid Evans was once an actor and invented the character of Brigadier Chatsworth to give himself an alibi whenever he needed one. Since he never knew when the compulsion would overtake him, he needed to have someone he could fall back on without notice.''

"Strange man. I always thought there was something odd about him. About them both, actually. But then they were both the same person. How very odd.''

"The odd thing about it was that I knew something wasn't right, but couldn't put my finger on it. I should have listened to the colonel. He swore he had never met Sid Evans, yet the man had complained about his war stories. "Evans must have forgotten that he was Chatsworth when the colonel talked to him."

"Quite a slip on his part."

"Fortescue also mentioned the fact that Brigadier Chatsworth talked about events during the Boer War that he knew nothing about. Of course, if Chatsworth had never been in the Boer War, he must have invented some stories to convince the colonel."

Baxter shook his head, as if trying to make sense of it all. "Well, I can understand why you didn't pay attention to Fortescue, bumbling old fool."

"Exactly, but there was something else to which I should have paid attention."

"What was that?"

Cecily breathed a long sigh. "It was the fiddling with the tie, of course. A nervous habit that isn't too strange in itself, but a little too much of a coincidence to ignore when two quite different men share the same habit."

"Of course." Baxter looked impressed. "I would never have noticed that."

"Then there was the fact that they didn't appear to have anything in common, yet seemed to spend a great deal of time together. Sid Evans's skin problem around his jaw was obviously a result of gluing a beard to it so often, and last of all, Sid Evans mispronounced my name. Last night, when we were talking to the brigadier, he did the same thing. I didn't notice at the time because I was upset about the murder, and I became confused as to which of them had pronounced it incorrectly before."

"I remember." Baxter frowned. "What I don't understand is why he didn't strangle you. I shall be eternally grateful that he didn't, of course, but it does seem rather strange that he came all the way up here to throw you off the roof."

Cecily shivered. She had been unconscious during that time, but the thought of how close she had come to losing her life was quite terrifying. "The inspector explained that.

As Dr. Prestwick had guessed, Sid Evans only strangled his victims when the compulsion was triggered by a certain set of events. In my case, there was no such trigger. He simply had to get rid of me because I knew too much. Inspector Cranshaw believes Evans was going to drop me from the roof in an attempt to make it look like an accident."

"Does anyone know why Sid Evans felt compelled to kill?"

Cecily shook her head. "I doubt if we shall ever know now."

"How extraordinary."

Something in his voice made her look closely at him. "What is it?"

"I was thinking about the first murder that occurred in this hotel. If I remember, it was a shoe button that led you to the culprit."

"Who eventually died in a fall from the roof."

"It would appear that we have come full circle."

She gazed silently out to sea for a long moment, then said quietly, "I just hope, for everyone's sake, but especially Edward's, that there will be no more tragedies in this hotel. If there is a curse on the Pennyfoot, perhaps it will be lifted once it has been remodeled."

"Well, I must say, I feel greatly relieved that you will no longer be chasing murderers through the hallways."

"I have to admit, Baxter, I shall rather miss all the excitement."

"Then we shall have to find something else to replace it."

She turned to him, feeling her spirits lift. "Such as a visit to Africa, for instance? I should dearly love to visit my grandson."

"The perfect spot for a honeymoon."

"Actually, I was thinking of emulating my son and arranging for a witch doctor to marry us in the jungle."

The look on his face drew a burst of laughter from her. "I was joking, Bax. I want to get married right here in Badgers End."

He groaned. "Don't tell me. St. Bartholomew's, with the reverend Algernon Carter-Holmes presiding."

"I think Madeline and Phoebe would make elegant maids-of-honor, don't you agree?"

He lifted his chin and clasped his hands behind his back. "Indubitably, madam."

She grinned. "I can't wait to hear whom you will pick for your best man."

"It won't be P.C. Northcott, I can promise you that."

She looked down at her hand, spreading out her fingers so that the sun glinted on the diamond. "I suppose we shall have to inform the staff right away. Edward wants to start the renovations next month to make the most of the good weather."

"We'll call a staff meeting in the ballroom after dinner tonight."

"This will be a shock for them all."

"They will be happy for us, I'm sure."

He'd sounded confident, but she couldn't help feeling just a little worried. "Things are changing so fast," she said a little wistfully. "It will be hard for the staff to adjust."

"No doubt, but as you are so fond of telling me, there is no progress without change. The entire world is changing, and we must learn to adapt with it." He reached for her hand and tucked it under his arm. "Come, my dear, let us go down and celebrate our betrothal with a bottle of our good French wine."

Cecily announced her coming marriage to Baxter that evening, standing with him on the ballroom stage and facing her delighted staff. A burst of applause greeted her words, with cries of good wishes echoing throughout the vast room.

Silence fell, however, when she informed her audience of the coming change of ownership. Most seemed reassured when she introduced Edward Sandringham, who promised everyone employment under the new management.

Descending from the stage, Cecily was surprised to see

Phoebe clinging to the arm of a beaming Colonel Fortescue.

"Darling Cecily," Phoebe cried, kissing the air on each side of Cecily's face, "what absolutely wonderful news. I am so very happy for you both."

"Thank you, Phoebe."

Colonel Fortescue grabbed Baxter's hand and pumped it up and down. "Congratulations, old chap! Got a good woman there, what? What?"

"I have indeed, Colonel," Baxter murmured, doing his best to extract his hand from the colonel's fierce grip.

"Darling, I absolutely hate to steal your thunder, but I also have an announcement to make." Phoebe simpered up at the colonel. "Frederick and I are to be married."

"Great Scott!" Baxter muttered.

Cecily gave him a discreet dig in the ribs. "That is marvelous news, Phoebe. I'm sure you'll be very happy."

Fortescue started pumping Baxter's hand again.

Ignoring him, Phoebe tilted forward and murmured, "Such a dreadful man, that brigadier. I knew at once, of course. You just can't trust men who are so very handsome and charming. Not like my Frederick. Now there's a man I can trust."

A somewhat backhanded compliment, Cecily thought in amusement. "Well, I do hope I shall be here for the wedding, Phoebe."

"If not, then you must come down for it. I trust you will be getting married at St. Bartholomews?"

"Of course. I'll pay a visit to Algie next week."

"He'll be delighted, I'm sure. Two weddings to preside over. How marvelous."

Cecily glanced at Baxter, who still struggled to remove his hand from the colonel's. "You will have to excuse us, Colonel," she said firmly. "We have business to attend to in the kitchen."

"Oh, of course, old girl. Jolly good luck and all that rot, what?"

"Thank you, Colonel. Until next week, Phoebe?"

Phoebe nodded, her hand clasping the colonel's arm to make him let go of Baxter. "Next week, then."

"Silly old fool," Baxter muttered as Cecily led the way across the ballroom. "I thought he was going to break my hand."

"He means well. He and Phoebe will be good for each other."

"I would have said they deserve each other."

"Come now, Bax. You can afford to be charitable, I would hope."

"If you say so. Where are we going?"

"To the kitchen. I must have a word with Mrs. Chubb."

He followed her to the kitchen, where she found everything in an uproar. As always, everyone seemed to be talking at once. Madeline stood in the middle of the room, holding James, while Daisy hugged Lilly in her arms.

Gertie was arguing with Mrs. Chubb, egged on by Michel, and Samuel leaned back against the sink taking huge bites out of a thick sandwich while he watched everyone else.

As Cecily entered, followed closely by Baxter, everyone gradually fell silent.

Mrs. Chubb bustled forward, tears glistening in her eyes. "I'm so happy for you, mum, and Mr. Baxter. Though it will be a sad day for us all when you leave."

Cecily reached for the housekeeper's hand. "What will you do, Mrs. Chubb? Edward is hoping you will stay on with him."

"Oh, I don't know, mum. I don't think I want to be around all those motorcar people. Too fast and noisy for me, they are."

"I've been bleeding telling her," Gertie said crossly. "Me and Ross are getting married and going back to Scotland to live. We want her to come with us and help with the babies."

Cecily looked at her in surprise. "That's wonderful, Gertie. I'm thrilled for you, though I must admit I'm surprised Ross is returning to Scotland."

"Yes, mum." Gertie looked guilty. "He has a business

there, you see. He came down here to ask me to marry him, and he was only going to stay until I agreed."

"I see." Cecily exchanged glances with Baxter. "Well, I wish you both well. You, too, Mrs. Chubb, if you decide to go with them."

"Of course she's bleeding coming with us," Gertie said fiercely. "Aren't you, Mrs. Chubb?"

"Yes, I think I am." The housekeeper yelped as Gertie joyfully flung her arms around her neck.

Madeline smiled. "All's well that ends well," she murmured. "Now the babies will have someone to take care of them."

Cecily stroked Lilly's soft head. "I trust my godchildren were on their best behavior while they were in your care?"

"They were absolute darlings." Madeline buried her mouth in the child's silky hair for a moment. "As a matter of fact, they made me realize what is missing in my life. I've decided it's time I had a child of my own."

Baxter looked startled. "Is that possible?"

Madeline uttered her silvery laugh. "I may have powers, Baxter, but I'm not a magician. I shall have to find a man to marry me, of course. Perhaps someone who knows more than I do about taking care of babies."

Cecily smiled, knowing she was referring to Dr. Prestwick. "I wish you well," she said, giving her friend a quick hug.

"Well, me and Samuel will be going to London," Daisy announced. She bounced the squirming James on her hip. "Doris is going to need us now that she's going to be famous."

"What about you, Michel?" Cecily looked across at the chef, who was doing his best to stay aloof of all the merriment.

"I am staying," he announced. "I do not desert ze ship when she sinks, *n'est ce pas*?"

"She ain't sinking." Samuel wiped his mouth with his sleeve. "She'll always be standing, won't she. No matter what they do to her, she'll always be the Pennyfoot to us. Nothing can change that.''

Cecily looked at Baxter, making no effort to hide her tears. ''Samuel's right,'' she said softly. ''The memories will always be with us, the happy times and the sad, and as long as we relive them now and again, the Pennyfoot Hotel will live on in our hearts forever.''

Baxter gave her a fond look, inclined his head, and murmured, ''Indubitably, madam.''

If you enjoy the Pennyfoot Hotel mystery series, you will also want to read *The Dumb Shall Sing,* by Stephen Lewis.

Catherine had just come out into the garden with Phyllis to see what vegetables might be gathered for supper when she heard a confused cacophony of voices rise from the road that skirted the hill on which her house sat. She and Phyllis hurried around to the front, and there she saw a crowd heading toward the northern edge of Newbury, where the town ran abruptly into the untamed woods. The voices seemed to carry an angry tone. She turned to Phyllis.

"Catch up with them, if you can, and see where they are going, and to what purpose."

She watched as the girl hurried down the hill and trotted toward the people, whose voices were becoming less distinct as they moved farther away. Catherine strained her eyes, keeping them focused on the white cap Phyllis wore, and she saw it bobbing up and down behind the crowd. The cap stopped moving next to a man's dark brown hat. After a few moments she could see the cap turn back toward her while the hat moved away, and shortly Phyllis stood before her, catching her breath.

"They are going to the Jameson house. They say the babe is dead. And they want you to come to say whether it was alive when it was born."

She recalled holding the babe in her arms and seeing that he was having trouble breathing. She had seen that his nose was clogged with mucus and fluids, and she had cleared it with a bit of rag she carried in her midwife's basket for that purpose. The babe had snorted in the air as soon as she removed the cloth and then he had bellowed a very strong and healthy cry. The only thing out of the ordinary during the birth that she could now remember was how the Jameson's Irish maidservant eyed the babe as though she wanted to do something with it. Catherine had seen dozens of births, and usually she could tell when a babe was in trouble. This one had given no indication of frailty.

"Come along with me, then," she said to Phyllis. "Just stop to tell Edward to watch for Matthew."

Phyllis did not respond, and Catherine motioned to the tree under which Massaquoit had slept.

"You know," Catherine repeated, "Matthew."

"I see, yes, he should wait for Matthew," Phyllis said.

"Edward need not think about going to lecture."

"He does not think about that anyway," Phyllis replied.

"Be that as it may, I do not think there will be lecture tonight," Catherine said. "Now go along with you."

The Jameson house was a humble structure of two sections, the older little more than a hut with walls of daub and wattle construction, a plaster of mud and manure layered over a substructure of crisscrossing poles. Henry Jameson had recently built a wing onto the back of the house to accommodate his growing family, and this new room was covered in wooden shingles outside and was generally more luxurious inside, having a wood plank floor and whitewashed plaster walls.

It was in this room that Martha had delivered her babe. Catherine remembered that the Irish servant girl had a little space, not much more than a closet, for a bed so that she could be near the infant's cradle, and that the parents' bedroom was in the original portion of the house. She also remembered how the girl had fashioned a crude cross out of two twigs, tied together with thread, and then hung it over her bed until Henry had found it there and pulled it off. He had taken the cross outside and ground it into the mud with the heavy heel of his shoe. There was a separate entrance to this side of the house, which gave onto a patch of wild strawberries, and it was before that door that the crowd had gathered.

As Catherine shouldered her way through the crowd, she felt hands grabbing at her sleeve. She was spun around, and for a moment she lost sight of Phyllis. Someone said, "I've got her," but Catherine pulled away. Phyllis emerged from behind the man who was holding Catherine's arm. A woman placed her face right in front of Catherine. She was missing her front teeth, and her breath was sour. She held a smoldering torch in one hand, and she brought it down near Catherine's face.

"Here, mistress," the woman said, "we've been waiting for you, we have."

Phyllis forced herself next to Catherine, shielding her from the woman.

"Go," Catherine said to Phyllis, "to Master Woolsey, and tell him to come here right away."

Phyllis pushed her way back through the crowd, which was advancing with a deliberate inevitability toward the house. Catherine moved with the energy of the crowd, but at a faster pace, so that soon she reached its leading edge, some ten or so feet away from Henry and Ned Jameson, who stood with their backs to their house. Ned had his arm around the Irish servant girl, flattening her breasts and squeezing her hard against his side. She held a pitcher in her hand. It was tilted toward the ground and water dripped from it. The girl's eyes were wide and starting as they found Catherine.

"Please," she said, but then Ned pulled her even harder

toward him, and whatever else the girl was trying to say
was lost in the breath exploding from her mouth.

The Jameson girls, ranging from a toddler to the oldest,
a twelve-year-old, were gathered around their mother, who
stood off to one side. Martha's gown was unlaced and one
heavy breast hung free as though she were about to give
her babe suck. Her eyes moved back and forth between her
husband and the crowd, seemingly unable or unwilling to
focus. The toddler amused itself by walking 'round and
'round through her mother's legs. The oldest girl seemed
to be whispering comfort to her younger siblings. Then the
girl turned to her mother and laced up her gown. Martha
looked at her daughter's hand as though it were a fly buzz-
ing about her, but she did not swipe it away.

Henry was holding the babe, wrapped in swaddling, and
unmoving. It was quite clearly dead. He took a step toward
Catherine and held out the babe toward her. His face
glowed red in the glare of a torch.

"Here she is," he shouted. He lowered his voice a little.
"Tell us, then, if you please, Mistress Williams, was this
babe born alive?"

"Who says nay?" Catherine asked. She looked at Martha, who stood mute, and then at the Irish servant girl, who
did not seem to understand what was happening. Always
the finger of blame, she thought, lands on some poor
woman while the men stand around pointing that finger
with self-righteous and hypocritical arrogance. She recalled
how Henry had asked first what sex the babe was before
he inquired as to his wife's health. "Henry will be glad,"
Martha had said as Catherine had held the babe in front of
her so that she could see its genitalia. And then Martha had
collapsed onto the bed, a woman exhausted by fifteen years
of being pregnant, giving birth, suffering miscarriages, and
nursing the babes that were born, and always there had been
the poverty. She had not wanted to take Ned in, for there
was never enough food.

"Just answer the question," Henry insisted. "We have
heard how soft your heart is for a savage. How is it with

this babe? Here, look at it, which is not breathing now who was when it was born. Was it not very much alive when you pulled it out of my wife's belly not three days ago?''

A voice came from the back of the crowd, strong, male, and insistent.

"An answer, mistress, we need to know the truth."

Catherine turned toward the voice, but she could not identify the speaker. It came from a knot of people that had gathered just beyond Ned in the shadow of a tall tree.

"The truth," the voice said again, and then was joined by other voices, male and female, rising from the group beneath the tree, and then spreading across the surface of the crowd like whitecaps in a storm-tossed sea. "The truth," they clamored, "tell us the truth."

"What says the mother, then?" Catherine demanded. "What says Goody Jameson?"

"Nothing," came the response from the group.

Catherine turned back to Henry.

"Your wife, Henry, what does she say?"

"Nothing," Henry repeated. "She no longer speaks. She came to me not an hour ago, holding the babe in her arms, and handed it to me, and she does not speak."

Catherine studied Martha's face. Its expression did not change as her children moved about her. She did not seem to see that her husband was holding her dead infant in his arms, and she did not hear the insistent cries for the truth. It was as though she were standing in a meadow daydreaming while butterflies circled her head. Every moment or two she extended her hand toward the toddler that clung to her knees, but the gesture was vague and inconsequential, and her hand never found her child's head.

Catherine stepped close to Martha, close enough to feel the woman's breath on her face.

"Martha, you must speak," Catherine said, and Martha's eyes now focused on her, as though she had just returned from that distant meadow. She shook her head, slowly at first, and then with increasing agitation. Catherine took Martha's shoulders in both hands and squeezed and then the nodding motion stopped. Still Martha did not speak.

"My poor wife is distracted by the death of our babe," Henry declared. "Can you not see that? Mistress Williams, you must answer for her."

"Well, then," Catherine said, "if Martha Jameson will not attest to the truth, I needs must say that this babe was born alive, and alive it was when I left it. Truth you want, and there it is."

A murmur arose from the crowd. It pushed toward Catherine.

"It is surely dead now," somebody said.

"If Goody Jameson won't speak, we have ways," said another.

"Yes, press her, stone by stone. She will talk, then, I warrant."

"You will leave her alone," Henry said, and the crowd, which had come within several feet of the clustered Jameson family, stopped. Henry held out the babe toward his wife.

"Tell them, Martha," he said. He thrust the babe toward her, but she did not hold out her arms to take it. He shook his head. "She brought the babe to me. It was dead. She said she had been asleep, and when she woke she saw the servant girl leaning over the babe. When she picked it up, it was not breathing. Then she brought it to me. That girl, she did something while my wife was asleep."

Catherine felt the anger rise in the crowd toward the servant. She remembered once, when she was a girl in Alford, how a crowd just like this one had fallen upon a little boy whose family was Catholic, and how they had beaten him with sticks until he lay senseless in the road. She strode to Ned and grabbed his arm.

"Let her go," she said.

"You are now interfering in my household, mistress. Leave be."

"Step away, mistress," a woman in the crowd said. "You have told us what we needed to know."

"She," Henry shouted, "standing there with the pitcher,

ask her what she was doing with our babe."

The servant girl turned her terrified and starting eyes toward her master. Their whites loomed preternaturally large in the failing light of the early evening.

"A priest, it was, I was after," she said.

Ned pushed the girl forward so she stood quivering in front of the crowd.

"That is it," he said, "that is how we found her, practicing her papist ritual on our babe, pouring water on its innocent face, and mumbling some words, a curse they must have been."

"Its poor soul," the girl muttered. "There was no priest. I asked for one. So I tried myself to save its precious soul."

Henry looked at his wife, whose eyes were now studying the ground at her feet. Then he stared hard at the girl, his face brightening as with a new understanding.

"You drowned it, for certain," he said. "Or you cast a spell on it so it could not breathe. What, a papist priest? In Newbury? You have killed our babe and driven my poor wife mad."

"Try her, then," came the voice from the knot of people, still grouped by the tree. "Have her touch the babe. Then we will know."

The crowd surged forward and Catherine found herself staggering toward Henry, who dropped to one knee against her weight. Henry threw one hand behind him to brace himself, and Catherine reached for the babe so as to stop it from falling. As she grabbed for it, its swaddling blanket fell. The babe's skin was cold. Henry regained his balance and wrapped the babe tightly in the blanket.

"Try her," again came the cry from the crowd.

"Surely not," Catherine said. "Magistrate Woolsey is coming. This is a matter for him."

"We need not wait for the magistrate. We will have our answer now," shouted one.

"Now," said another.

"Right," said Ned. "We will try her now."

Catherine turned to face the crowd and to peer over it to

the road, where day was giving way to dusk. She thought
she saw two figures approaching.

"The magistrate is coming even now," she said.

Henry looked at Ned, and the boy pushed the servant girl
toward him.

"Touch the babe," Ned demanded.

"Yes, touch it," Henry said. "If it bleed, it cries out
against you."

"There is no need for that," Catherine said. "Talk of
the dead bleeding. It is surely blasphemy."

"The blood will talk," came a voice from a crowd.

"Yes," others confirmed, "let the poor dead babe's
blood cry out against its murderer."

The girl clasped her arms in front of her chest, but Ned
pulled her hands out. She struggled, but he was too strong,
and he was able to bring one hand to the exposed skin of
the babe's chest. He pressed the hand onto the skin, and
then let her pull her hand back. Henry peered at the spot
she had touched, and then lifted the babe over his head in
a triumphant gesture.

"It bleeds," he said. "It bleeds."

He held the babe out for the crowd to see. Catherine
strained her eyes as Henry and the babe were now in shadows. Henry turned so that all could view. Catherine was
not sure she saw blood on the babe's chest, but something
on its back caught her eye, and then she could no longer
see.

"Blood," cried voices in the crowd. "The babe bleeds!
Seize her!"

There was a violent surge forward, and Catherine felt
herself being thrown to the ground. She got to her feet just
in time to see rough hands grabbing the servant girl and
pulling her away. . . .